MOON ANGEL

////

J.R. RAIN

THE VAMPIRE FOR HIRE SERIES

Published by
Crop Circle Books
212 Third Crater, Moon

Printed in the United States of America.

ISBN-13: 978-1548255190
ISBN-10: 154825519X

Dedication
To Mr. Hogue.

1.

"But how are we going to find her, Sam?" asked Allison.

"They're connected, somehow," I said. "She let him in."

My words hung in the air. I saw my friends look at each other.

"Possession?" asked Kingsley.

Both of my friends knew the devil had been here yesterday—the devil and his three-headed dog. They also knew my son, who was presently standing in the hallway and holding his sister's cell phone, which had been left behind, had shifted into what we lovingly, teasingly and admiringly called the Fire Warrior —a giant, fiery, interdimensional being. My son had, of course, taken care of one of the devil dog's heads by lopping it right off. The devil, who had apparently come for my son, had, instead, turned his sights to my daughter; at least, that was what I had pieced together.

Unfortunately, I didn't have access to my daughter's mind, nor my son's. But shortly thereafter, as witnessed by me, Tammy had seemed a little too quick to defend the devil, and a little moodier than normal. She'd been oddly quiet too, and my every instinct told me that she had made a connection with the devil. That dirty piece-of-shit devil.

Allison was nodding. "A mindlink."

"Somehow, the devil enticed her," said Kingsley. "Or awakened something within her."

"Awakened what?" I snapped.

Kingsley knew he was treading on dangerous ground, but he plowed forward anyway. "Something that's within all of us: darkness. The devil, I'm willing to bet, knows how to coax such darkness out of people."

What sort of darkness had been in Tammy? What could the devil have possibly coaxed out? I didn't know, but I knew my daughter had seen into the minds of some terrible, no-good, very bad people. And these were just everyday people she passed on the streets, or crossed paths with in stores, or in school. I knew the odds of her coming across a vile and terrible person increased with each day of her existence. And she had the uncanny ability to easily and swiftly pop into and out of such minds. She rarely talked about what she saw, but I suspected she had seen some crazy shit—my own family and friends included. Tammy would put on a brave face, but a few times, I had seen the confusion, the fear, the sense of innocence lost.

She was only sixteen. Had she been forever traumatized? Hell, even good people had their own inner demons. Tammy had seen it all. And she continued seeing it, day after day. Yes, there was darkness in her. There had to be. Some of what she had seen scared her, confused her, tempted her, and the devil had awakened it now.

After all, that's what the bastard did. He encouraged darkness. He encouraged misdeeds. The bastard took an active, gleeful role in promoting the very darkness that caused belief in him. Job security, I guess.

And now, the piece of shit had set his eyes on my kids—in particular, Tammy. Anyone would have been interested in Tammy. Hell, what law enforcement agency, from the local PD to the most secretive shadow agencies in the government, wouldn't have use for her? They all would, and that scared the shit out of me.

Then again, what CIA covert operation wouldn't want Allison by its side, blasting through doors? Or Talos, the ultimate drone, scouting enemy terrain? Yes, they all would. But my daughter... oh, yes, she would be particularly prized. To know what the enemy was thinking was priceless.

I paced some more, running my fingernails through my hair. Yes, the devil saw her potential and formed a mindlink with her because he could. An idea hit me. "Allie, can you still do remote viewing?"

"I can," she began, then shook her head. "But I've only done it on the phone, when talking to my clients and I've been taking so much time off."

Her customers were, of course, those who called her psychic hotline. And, yes, she had been taking time off to hunt her own brand of bad guys with her witchy trifecta.

"Good idea, Sam," said Kingsley, who had been at this supernatural game longer than we had. "Allie, you need only to establish a connection yourself. Sam, grab something important to Tammy. A shirt, shoes, something."

Anthony held up Tammy's phone. "Her most important possession on Earth."

We could all only agree.

Allison took it and held it loosely in her hands. Back in the day, I would have had a peek inside her mind. But now... nothing, thanks to Millicent, a one-time friend of mine in a past life who now didn't trust me with the trifecta's innermost secrets. Fine, whatever. They could have their damn secrets.

"I can sort of feel her, Sam," reported Allison after what seemed like minutes, but had, in reality, been only a few seconds. "I mean, I can feel her attachment to this phone, as if it were a living thing. I can see thread-like strands crisscrossing the phone, strands that attach to her."

"The strands," I said, "how far do they reach?"

She blinked at me. "I don't know."

"All the way to her?" asked Kingsley.

"Let me see what I can see," said Allison, and now, she turned her head a little. "They reach all the way to her, Sam. I can feel her. Yes, she wishes she had her phone now. But the devil told her to leave it."

"Do you see her?" I asked. "Is she okay? Is she afraid? Is she with someone?"

"Hold on."

Shit, I held on the best I could, but I was fucking losing it. So, I held on to Kingsley, who held me, too, and we stood like that in my little foyer while Allison held the phone and turned her head this way and that. Finally, she opened her eyes, and looked at me.

"She's in Santa Ana."

"Santa Ana?" And then, it hit me. Yesterday, Tammy had mentioned Santa Ana. In particular, she had mentioned the jogger who had been forced to work as a prostitute in Santa Ana.

A jogger who had been possessed by the devil.

I grabbed my keys. "Let's go."

2.

Tammy didn't particularly like the devil.

She knew what he had made that handsome biker do a few months ago. She had seen it all in her mother's memories: the man stepping backward onto the train track and his body veritably exploding into a bloody mist, complete with flying chunks of meat. Tammy thought she used the word "veritably" correctly, but she would have to look it up later. She liked looking up words. Words helped her explain what she saw in people's minds, and what she saw often confused her, although the confusion seemed to be getting less and less these days. After all, the question was: what had she *not* seen at this point?

Going through a rundown of what she had seen would almost certainly guarantee to put her in a bad mood, or to depress her so much that all she would want to do was eat. She had to be careful with that, she knew. She turned to eating to feel good, and she thought it might turn into a problem. Then again, eating really did help her feel good, so who cared what other people thought?

Now, as she made her way along busy Bristol Avenue in downtown Santa Ana, she could feel the devil nearby. No, not really feel him. She could *see* the devil nearby. In her mind. Hear him too. Or hear *her*, since the devil was still possessing the body of the female jogger. But the female jogger wasn't jogging now, was she?

Nope, not at all. As Tammy walked, she mentally looked on in fascination, and then decided she'd seen enough. Maybe even too much.

Yes, definitely too much.

The devil was making the woman perform tricks in nearby cars. Tammy knew that tricks meant sex for money, and it revolted her, but yet, like all things that she saw, it fascinated her up to a point.

The woman had worshiped the devil.

Tammy could see that. Tammy could see pretty deeply into the woman's mind, too, especially now that the woman, she was sure, was right around the corner, in a truck, doing things for money against her will, because the devil controlled her every action.

The devil, as far as Tammy could tell, was a real douche.

Now, as she walked along the street at night, knowing that she was garnering the looks of the wayward males in the area, many of whom were drunk or high and mostly harmless, she could see more into the woman, who, deep down, was scared. She was horrified, too. She was certain she had gotten a venereal disease, and she hated the devil. She hated the devil for making her do this. She was also, perversely, honored that the devil had chosen her. But the part that felt honored was drowning quickly in a sea of nastiness. The woman knew she was in trouble. She knew she had lost control of her body by letting in the devil. She had let him in willingly, too, through a blood sacrifice that involved small animals and her own blood.

Tammy could hear her screaming in her own head. But she was trapped, buried beneath the weight of that which possessed her. She sensed Tammy watching her and she shifted her attention toward her, begging Tammy to help her—and Tammy jumped out of her mind. She had seen enough.

Tammy wasn't entirely sure why she came out tonight, or why she had slipped inside Kingsley's mind—yet again—but this time, to give him the suggestion to sleep. Tammy hadn't thought it could work, but it did work. All the big guy needed was a simple suggestion, placed deep enough into his subconscious, and that suggestion bubbled up to the surface as a real need to sleep. He hadn't been sleepy before. In fact, he had been working pretty hard on notes for his new case, a case that had bored her to no end, which was why she had mostly stayed out of his head.

Until she heard the devil beckoning.

Tammy knew she could keep him out of her head, if she wanted to. The cool thing about all this mind reading was that she had taught herself how to protect her own mind in ways that she knew, without a doubt, that no one, but no one could have access to it. For instance, she knew how to seal up her mind, wall it off, block it. But the devil had figured a way to connect with her anyway. To call to her. It wasn't much, but she heard it. And it had all happened yesterday. She suspected that once she had slipped inside the devil's mind, a sort of trap had been sprung. Kind of like opening an email virus. But she knew how minds worked, and how to access them, and she knew, roughly, where the connection lay in her mind. She also knew that she could remove it when she wanted to. Or so she hoped.

And so, she had put Kingsley to sleep and taken a bus. A few dozen stops later and here she was, walking the streets of Santa Ana, knowing the devil was just around the corner.

She felt excited, nervous and curious. And now that she could offer people suggestions— especially those people who might want to do her harm—she could do more than just avoid them. She could possibly control them too.

Tammy turned a corner and recognized the woman who stepped out of a car with steamed-up windows as the same jogger from the day before. Tammy had known it would be her, of course. Heck, Tammy had been connected to her since yesterday.

How much of the devil was inside her, Tammy didn't know. Maybe it was only a part of him. Maybe the devil possessed many dozens or hundreds of people around the world. Tammy didn't know. If so, she had never come across him in any other mind. Indeed, this was a new experience for her.

The woman adjusted her short skirt and the man behind the wheel drove off. A quick scan of his mind and Tammy knew all about his cheating ways, his self-hate, his guilt, his depression, his suicidal thoughts. She also saw that he was an important man, a rich man. He was a politician of some sort. A congressman. She saw the devil's hold on the man. Tammy knew the man had, in essence, sold his soul to the devil. The man knew it, but didn't know it, too. Tammy had seen something similar, when her mother had inadvertently turned that handsome boxer into a sex slave. So gross, but so damn interesting too. The devil, she knew, had created a similar attachment within the congressman. But unlike her mother, who had released the boxer, the devil sought to use the man. Use and abuse him. The congressman knew it on some level, too, but he didn't care. The man only wanted to please the devil, in whatever form the devil took. At this point, the man did not care if the devil possessed a man or a woman. He needed the connection. He needed to please, no matter what... forever.

Tammy stood before the woman. She had a nice figure and was pretty enough. But her lipstick was smeared, and her hair was tangled and dirty.

Unlike her mother, whose entity existed deep beneath her consciousness, Tammy could see the devil right there, front and center in the woman's mind. It was, in fact, the woman who was buried deep below. Tammy could see that the devil had big plans for this woman. He planned to use her to bring many powerful men to their knees, to blackmail them and use them and hopefully destroy them and those around them. Or he might just kill her. He hadn't decided which.

"You heard my call," said the woman—said the devil—wiping the back of her hand across her face, smudging the lipstick even farther across her cheek. She looked psychotic.

Tammy wrapped her arms around herself. She tried telling herself that it was cold—and it was, kinda—but she suddenly realized just how far away from home she was, and how far away her mother was too.

Now Tammy heard other voices, whisperings that seemed to come from everywhere and anywhere, from the shadows in the alley, from the shadows under cars and in corners, on the cold wind, too, and all of which seemed to be coming to a head here, in this place, around this woman with lipstick smeared across her face.

In fact, yes, the whispering seemed to be swirling around them, swirling and swirling, and the woman before her—especially the entity within—seemed to be highly attuned to all the whisperings. More than that, it seemed to be responding to the whisperings, on another, higher level that even Tammy couldn't quite penetrate. At least, not yet. It seemed—yes, it seemed as if the entity before her had delegated a part of itself to constantly, continuously, effortlessly, responding to the whisperings—no, to the information—that was coming to it. So, in a way, the thing before her could both focus on Tammy, but also give a part of itself to running what Tammy assumed was a very dark and terrible empire of fear.

Tammy could almost, almost, make out the whisperings. She thought she caught a snatch of "...is ready now" and "...has killed again." Tammy couldn't see where the voices were coming from, not exactly, but out of the corner of her mind, she sensed movement... shadowy figures just beyond her perception.

"There's a lot going on in that mind of *yoursss*, child," said the woman, her voice veritably hissing, but not quite in the way the dark masters hissed when they spoke to her mother. The thing was, Tammy wasn't one hundred percent certain the woman had spoken the words. They might have just as easily been projected to her.

"I'm not a child," said Tammy.

"Then what are you?" asked the devil.

Tammy thought about that. She didn't feel like an adult, not yet anyway, but she certainly didn't feel like a child. She said, "I'm just not a child, okay?"

"Fair enough," said the devil, and now, Tammy could hear what sounded like a low growl in the voice. In fact, the voice was sounding less like a woman, and more like an angry man.

"Not angry," said the devil. "Let's just say, I'm passionate."

"About what?" asked Tammy. She noticed that the street was nearly empty. She also noticed, from the corners of her eyes, shadowy movement.

"A good question, lass," said the devil. Tammy knew the word 'lass.' Jacky the boxer called her mother a lass, and Tammy always kind of liked it, too, even though she knew it was, like, Irish for 'girl.'

Better than 'child,' she thought. And as she thought that, she suspected the devil had plumbed that information from deep within her memory bank. Yes, he was inside her head, but he wasn't so deep inside that he could see the secret she was carrying. A secret she had boxed up nicely. A secret that she knew the devil would have reacted to, had he seen it.

Yes, thought Tammy in this secret place

inside her mind. *He can't reach everywhere.*

Which was a relief to her.

The devil watched her curiously, and Tammy knew he sensed he was missing something, that something was being, in fact, hidden from him, and this made him angrier and more curious.

The devil said, "I am passionate about my work, you could say. I am passionate about my continued existence."

The woman stepped forward. Her movements seemed odd, her steps too long, her arms too stiff. She looked like a praying mantis or something. Tammy sensed the devil's confusion. She also sensed the devil's rage. It was welling up and it was terrible. Tammy was pretty sure she had never seen pure evil before, until now. Right there inside the woman's mind, burning white and hot—and also black and slimy.

The devil was still next to her ear. In fact, she could feel the woman's longish hair brushing against her neck, a sensation that made Tammy's skin crawl. The devil cocked her head this way and that, as if trying to get a look inside Tammy's ear.

More shadows shifted and moved around Tammy, and she had a sudden insight. "It was the shadows who summoned me, not you. The shadows formed a sort of chain, all the way to my house, because shadows are everywhere, aren't they? And the things you control live in the shadows."

"Is that right, now?" asked the devil.

"Yes, I think it is right. You need help. Lots of help. You are not as powerful as you want us all to believe."

The woman stepped around and stood before her again. Tammy was pleased that her words had gotten to the devil, who seethed now just inside the woman's mind. If anything, the hate glowed brighter and darker, something Tammy had never seen before: bright and dark occupying the same space.

"There is a space in your mind, a hidden space," said the devil, who now sounded nothing like the woman. "You are hiding a secret from me."

"A girl needs her secrets," said Tammy, feeling a lot more confident than she probably should.

Tammy sensed within the devil real confusion and a lot of anger. The devil was not used to mortals keeping secrets from him. Immortals, yes. The devil, like most immortals, could not penetrate the minds of other immortals. He hadn't been able to penetrate her mother's mind, nor had her mother been able to penetrate his. Tammy could penetrate it—and could go quite deep if she chose. She chose not to. Digging inside that mind, she suspected, would lead to madness.

"I will find your secrets, lass. For now, let me tell you a story. Once upon a time, there was a little, pesky vampire who had proven to be particularly troublesome to the dark masters. The dark masters thought they could control her. They thought wrong. They began realizing this vampire bitch—sorry, your mother—was more trouble than she was worth. They began to realize that they might need to find another. Do you know what 'jump ship' means?"

3.

I was driving my minivan. I hung a right, then a left, and gunned it down a mostly empty street. I ran a red light, then blew through a stop sign, and nearly hit a young man wearing earbuds in a crosswalk who didn't seem too happy about it.

"Where next?" I asked, picking up speed on a busy street, weaving past slow-moving cars that were going the speed limit. I cursed them and panicked and, quite frankly, barely remembered any of it.

Allie pointed northwest, and I continued zig-zagging through the city, since there wasn't a street that angled northwest. That was, until we came across Anaheim Street, which cut diagonally and gloriously through the city.

I gunned the minivan as fast as it would go, which wasn't nearly fast enough for my taste.

"She's with a woman," said Allison between whimpers. "A really messed-up looking woman."

"Messed-up, how?"

"Lipstick smeared on her face, hair in disarray. She's sort of walking around Tammy, talking to her, touching Tammy's hair sometimes."

I gripped the steering wheel hard enough to tear the faux-leather covering. Touching my daughter? That thought alone caused me to blow through a red light. Hey, my inner alarm hadn't sounded, and I knew we would be safe. Then again, they didn't know that.

"Who is she, Sam?" asked Allison, next to me. "The jogger from yesterday?"

"Would be my guess."

She didn't have to say it. None of us had to say it. We all knew the jogger from yesterday was the devil himself.

I blew through another red light.

***

"The dark masters are very, very serious about re-emerging into this world, lass. But your mother isn't cooperating and they are losing patience."

Tammy nearly asked how the devil knew this, but knew that was a stupid question. The devil had shadowy agents everywhere. Literally, everywhere.

"Well, tough shit," said Tammy, feeling her spine stiffen. "My mom's immortal. And Elizabeth is stuck. Forever. And from what I understand, they need Elizabeth to carry out their plan."

"All true, child, except you and I both know that a vampire *can* die."

The words hung in the air, words that Tammy knew but didn't want to acknowledge.

"In short, they are planning your mother's execution. They are planning it carefully and, once done, Elizabeth will be free to pursue her next target. And in case you don't know where I'm going with this, that next target is you. Granted, you are not ideal, but they think they can make it work."

"I'll never help them! And Mommy will never die, either. She's smarter than them, tougher than them. They'll never hurt her."

"Perhaps, perhaps not. Your mother, as you know, lost her guardian angel. Your mother, quite frankly, has been left without protection."

"What are you saying?" asked Tammy.

The woman spread her hands wide. "I will offer her my protection. After all, it behooves me to keep the dark masters at bay. There is, after all, only room for one sheriff in town."

"In exchange for what?"

"Your mind, of course," said the devil. "Now, do we have a deal?"

***

"Down this street, Sam. There, do you see her?"

I did. She was standing under a streetlamp with a woman who appeared to be wearing clown makeup in front of a closed pizza joint. I noticed other things too: my inner alarm sounding, the street being oddly devoid of foot and car traffic, and the moving shadows... yes, the many shadows that seemed to be crawling up street poles or swirling under cars. Shadows that flitted through the air like black flags. I nearly rubbed my eyes, but I didn't have to. I knew these were living shadows, dark souls, an aspect which had been left behind on Earth, while the majority of them burned in hell. I'd always suspected these forgotten, lost fragments stuck around to help the devil, seeking forgiveness. After all, why help the very entity responsible for one's seemingly eternal punishment? I didn't know, but it was a sick circle, and here was my daughter in the middle of it.

"Sam, that woman—"

"—is the devil," I said. "Hang on."

***

Tammy gasped, turned her head.

She'd been hearing her mother for quite some time, but she'd been keeping that knowledge in that secret corner of her brain. But the minivan roaring down the center of the street was hard to deny.

The woman looked, too, and grinned. "Mommy's here. I would say 'just in time' but you and I know both know different, don't we, Lady Tam Tam? You and I both know that your mother arrived just a fraction too late."

"You will protect her, right?" asked Tammy. "You will keep her safe? You will keep an eye on her, like you promised?"

"Oh, I will keep my eye on her, don't you worry. Meanwhile, you will be hearing from me again soon. I have some work for you."

With that, the woman calmly reached inside her purse and removed a handgun. And with the minivan nearly on top of them, she placed the barrel of the gun next to her temple. The woman's eyes flashed with real fear and Tammy knew she was looking at the real woman, not the devil. Except the real woman couldn't control herself, not even a little bit. She had just mouthed, "Help me." Then the side of her head blew off.

Tammy screamed and kept on screaming as she watched an oily, slithery, wet shadow rise up out of the dead woman and into the air. It rose higher and higher and disappeared.

4.

"Tammy's in her room," said Allie, looking up from the TV. I was pleased to see she was watching *Judge Judy*.

"It was the only thing on."

"I'm rubbing off on you," I said, and plopped down on the couch next to her. It was midday, the usual time I woke up, except my kids had stayed home today at my insistence. No surprise there. With Allie here, I could have slept in. Except the devil had his eye on my kids, and that made sleeping in damn near impossible.

He had to be stopped. Just how, I didn't know. Not yet.

For now, I still needed to wake up.

We'd spent most of the last night answering questions from the police, who I had telepathically convinced to leave us out of their reports. Of course, there was no denying that my daughter would show up on CCTV footage talking to the woman. There was also no good reason for my daughter to have been in Santa Ana in the middle of the night. So, I had told them that my daughter had run away. Again.

The dead woman had been looking for someone to talk to. The dead woman, it turned out, had been a realtor in Huntington Beach. A very successful realtor. Well, the police were about to discover that some people could sink to new lows. (Just wait until they saw her emerging from car after car, turning trick after trick.)

I left the devil out of it, of course. So did my daughter. Then again, she'd spent the night crying in my minivan. Allie and I had taken turns holding her hand. With each sob, I found myself growing angrier and angrier with the devil. Tammy had finally admitted that the devil had coerced her into making a deal with him, that he'd convinced her that my life was in danger from the dark masters, that they would, in fact, seek another. To do so meant that Elizabeth would have to be free. In order for her to be freed, that meant I would have to be dead.

Whether his information was correct or not, the devil had frightened Tammy into making a deal with him.

"Thank you again for watching them," I said, drinking my coffee and sitting across from her on my L-shaped couch. She'd stayed with my kids all day. At this rate, I was going to have to homeschool my kids.

"Of course, Sam. She slept for most of the day. Anthony has been in and out of his room, playing video games and watching TV. I tried to get him to do his homework and he said he would. I'm pretty sure he hasn't."

I nodded absently. Anthony and homework didn't mix, but I knew he did his best. I also knew that Allison had to cancel all her personal training appointments today, and call in sick for her psychic hotline job—although she could do that from anywhere, just as long as she had a laptop and Internet connection. Of course, she had previously made it known that she felt self-conscious doing it here. Mostly because she had heard me make fun of her from the kitchen.

"You've gone over and above the call of duty. I'll make it up to you somehow."

"Just knowing you guys are safe is enough."

Indeed, having Allie watching over my kids had been comforting. My best friend's powers seemed to only be growing. Or, more likely, she was learning how to control them better.

"A little bit of both," she said, picking up on my thoughts.

I nodded. Kingsley was in court today. A big case. He had set off for home in the wee hours of the morning, after sitting by my side all night, holding my hand. He was dealing with his own guilt for letting Tammy slip past him. I reminded him that my daughter wasn't just anyone, and she probably could have put any of us to sleep with her power of suggestion. My daughter's own mental prowess, I feared, was growing. And now, the devil had access to it.

I said to Allison, "Can you give us a shield?"

"I can," said Allison, "but it weakens in minutes. Or, rather, she finds a way through it within minutes."

"Good enough," I said.

Allison nodded, closed her eyes and raised her hands a little, palms up. And, son-of-a-bitch, if the air around us didn't suddenly shimmer, like heat rising up from an oasis. But in this case, I knew it was a bubble of silence that surrounded us—and kept out the sound too. She and I might as well have been in a soundproof studio.

"Even better," she said, picking up my thoughts. "What's on your mind?"

"The devil has his claws in my daughter."

"They're connected," said Allie.

I knew it wasn't possession, but it was damn near close. Their mindlink gave him access to her and, according to my daughter, he didn't need to be close by. He could use a chain of shadowy entities to reach her, from anywhere. To whisper suggestions to her. In essence, my daughter would never be free of the devil.

"And I can't have that," I said, finishing my thought with words, knowing Allison would have been following along.

"But, Sam. She made a deal with the devil. Isn't that the same as selling your soul?"

I shook my head. "Selling one's soul is just that: offering one's soul in exchange for a favor."

"She offered her services in exchange for your protection."

"Yes, but not her soul."

"No, but she offered her mind."

Something clenched my gut.

"But how binding is it?" asked Allison. "I mean, she's only sixteen, and he scared her into doing it."

"I don't know," I said. "I could give a shit if it's binding."

Allie was silent, even if *Judge Judy* wasn't. Allie was up to her old self, and I just wanted to sink into the couch and forget the devil had ever come knocking—and somehow forget, too, that Anthony's underwear needed washing. His boxers were in the laundry room in the garage, looking like the world's most dangerous intersection, skid marks and all.

"Gross, Sam," said Allie.

"You don't have to listen to everything."

"That went south faster than I could pull out of your head. He's old enough to do his own laundry now, you know."

I nodded. He was. But was I ready to admit he was? I liked having a little boy to take care of.

Allie said, "And do you really need protecting? Are the dark masters really hunting you?"

"I don't know," I said. It didn't ring true to me. If anything, I was getting along better than ever with Elizabeth. Granted, we weren't besties, but I didn't have a strong sense that she was trying to take over my body. And if she was, she was keeping it to herself. Unfortunately, I couldn't read her mind, although she could read the hell out of mine, which I didn't think was very fair, but I didn't make the rules. Kingsley had once had suggested that maybe her own mind might reside in the Void, that parallel world they'd been banished to. That what I was sensing was only an aspect of her, a fragment. I didn't know, and I never asked. Other than me keeping her sealed away in the deepest reaches of my mind, I wasn't aware of any animosity. I always knew that my resistance to her had slowed the dark masters' plans. Hell, maybe even ground them to a halt. So, yeah, it did make sense for them to someday give up on me. Unfortunately for them, I didn't plan on dying anytime soon.

I shook my head at the craziness of it all. Just over a decade ago, my life had been normal, happy, safe, secure... peaceful. Now, I didn't know what to make of it.

"Sam," said Allison, interrupting my pity party. "Have you ever considered the fact that you knew you were going to be turned into a vampire in this life, that you knew you were going to host a key dark master?"

"Where's this coming from?"

"I'm just thinking out loud. I'd read that before our births, we sort of knew what we were getting into, that we had been given a glimpse of our future lives."

"What are you getting at?"

She turned to me, tucking her sock-clad feet under her. "I think you knew all of this was going to happen, and you accepted it."

"Accepted what, exactly?"

"The responsibility of protecting everyone. Sam, think about it. If you knew that you were going to be a vampire—and potentially host one of the most powerful of the dark masters—then you did so willingly."

"What are you saying?"

"Yes, your life was normal a while ago, but there was a greater evil on the horizon, an evil that desperately wants back into this world. You, and you alone, have kept it at bay. And you accepted the responsibility. Sam, you are the gatekeeper. This is a challenge that you willingly took on."

"I didn't willingly ask to be attacked, Allie," I said.

"No, but you knew you would, at the soul level. And you came here anyway. You accepted the assignment, so to speak."

"What are you saying?" I asked.

"You knew you were tough enough to handle them. And you are tough enough to handle them now."

I considered her words, then recalled what my daughter had told me last. "The devil said there was only enough room for one sheriff in town. What did he mean?"

"Maybe he sees the dark masters as a threat?"

"But I thought the bastard *liked* when people

wreaked havoc in the world. And the dark masters have wreaked the most havoc of all."

"What if he meant there was only enough room for one ultimate evil? After all, what if the world began to fear the dark masters, and not him? Wouldn't he lose relevance?"

I knew a lot of the devil's existence was predicated on people's belief in him. Part of that belief was a belief in hell itself, of which the devil was intricately a part.

"I don't know," I said.

"Then who could be the 'other sheriff' he's worried about?"

"I don't know that either," I said.

I knew that something had to give here. The devil had caused Danny to flee and hide in my son. True, the devil had helped my son—with an implied favor owed. He had mind-linked with my daughter—and then blackmailed her to make a pact with him. The devil had sowed seeds of hate and destruction the world over, for centuries, if not millenniums. The devil, as far as I was concerned, had to go.

"Go, how?" asked Allison.

"I don't know," I said. "But first things first. I need to speak to Elizabeth."

5.

I was in my home office at the back of the house, sitting in what I had once thought was a fairly comfortable recliner, until I was informed recently by Allison that it was, in fact, a Spirit Chair. Funny, the guys at La-Z-Boy never mentioned that.

It sat in the far corner of my office, with my sliding glass door on one side, a bookcase on the other, and a little catch-all table next to it, which was piled with more books, empty coffee cups, and a water bottle or three. Yes, I cleaned the table before any clients came by. I hadn't had a client in a week. In fact, Charlie Reed had been my last official client.

Now, with Allison resuming *Judge Judy*, and with my daughter presumably asleep in her bedroom, I got comfortable in the recliner and closed my eyes. Sure, both Allie and Tammy could undoubtedly read my thoughts, and I wasn't receiving anything close to privacy, the truth of the matter was, they were going to hear about my conversation with Elizabeth anyway. Truth was, my brain was open season for both of them. And the Alchemist, for that matter. Oh, and Elizabeth.

I sighed and got even more comfortable, burrowing my ass deeper into the seat cushion. My overhead fan was on, whirring just loud enough to give me the background noise I needed to drown out Allie, and to drown out Anthony, who was laughing at whatever show he was watching, and occasionally slapping the floor as he was wont to do. Meditating in a house full of kids—and your friendly neighborhood witch—was never going to be truly quiet. I settled for peaceful.

I took some deep breaths, and mentally prepared myself for what was to come. Bringing forward the entity within me wasn't a hard thing to do. I didn't need the kind of concentration I needed for automatic writing, or having an inner dialogue with Gaia, the Earth Mother. No, Elizabeth was always there, always waiting.

And she came forth eagerly. Hell, the moment I thought her name, I felt her surging up from the depths, racing through the various roadblocks that I'd put in place to keep her down, and now, here she was, in the center of my thoughts, front and center.

Good afternoon, Sssamantha Moon, she said, hissing slightly. Why she hissed, I didn't know. But they all did it. I suspected it was meant to disarm and alarm, to cause confusion and fear.

You know us well, Sssamantha.

Well, just cool it. You and I have been at this for a while. You can't scare me.

Not true.

I thought about that, then nodded. Indeed, letting her out *did* scare me. Terrified me, even. I did not want to be relegated to the shadows. I did not want to lose control of myself, and give her any control. Which brought me back to my question.

Talk to me about the plot against me.

There was a small pause before her words came to me. *There is no plot against you, Moon Dance.*

Oddly enough, I believed her. In fact, I felt the truth of her words. Generally, I thought of her as a wispy, shadowy, formless, thoughtless being. A waif, a shade. A non-human entity. I even thought of her as a demon at times. All of which made little sense; after all, I spoke often to her very own son, Archibald Maximus. I mean, I knew she was a mother. Or had been a mother.

With that said, yes, her mind was elusive to me, and my own daughter's inability to read her only seemed to reinforce the idea that there was not much to this woman, at least, not much left. But now, as I sought her truth, as I felt more connected to her than I had in a long, long time, I also saw more of her too. She seemed to expand before me. Come to life before me. I sensed her own fear and confusion at being stifled for over a decade. Then again, I was not sorry I had done so. She really was someone to fear, and she really did want to take over my body. Not to mention, none of this was my idea.

But according to Allison, I might have very well known what I was getting into this mess. Enough to hurt anyone's head.

I caught another thought from Elizabeth. She did not want to take over my body, not any more. No, she had resigned herself to living in the shadows and only hoped for a few minutes of air time here and there. Perhaps once a month —hell, once a year. She would take anything I gave her.

The problem was, I knew if I gave her even

an inch, she would take a mile. The doorway would be forever open. The Alchemist had warned me that there was no turning back once that happened. Once open, the doorway stayed open.

I sensed her wanting to object, but she couldn't.

Then it's true, I thought. *If I ever did let you out, you would take over more and more.*

She didn't want to answer, but I already sensed the answer in her, anyway.

It is true, Sssamantha. It is the way of possession. Does the chick not want to break free from the egg? Does the sea turtle not crawl instinctively to the sea? We all want freedom.

And yet you chose bondage?

We can be so free as to choose bondage, Sssamantha.

I felt more truths within her, and thought, *You did not know I would be such a hard-ass.*

I would have said 'worthy adversary' but yes, came her response.

You thought you would control me by now.

Yes and no, Moon Dance. I knew you were strong. I knew your bloodline was strong. I knew you were a formidable witch—

How in the hell would you know about my past lives? I barely even remember them.

And what memory I had was fleeting at best.

It is not so hard to access the Akashic Records, child. They are there for all to read, between lives.

I knew about these records, of course. *The Book of Life*, as it was sometimes called. A recording of all our lives, throughout all of time.

That doesn't explain how you knew I would be born to my parents, at this time, a convergence of my witchy past... and the bloodline I would be born into in this life.

Many lives, Sssamantha. You often choose this bloodline, although not always. It is a rich and powerful and formidable bloodline, and always, it has helped sharpen and hone your witchcraft. All should be so lucky to be born from the great Hermetic bloodline.

Let's focus here, I thought. *That still does not explain how you knew I would be here, in this place, at this time.*

That is not my secret to tell, she responded.

Fine, I thought. *Tell me about the plot against me.*

There is no plot, Sssamantha.

It makes sense for there to be one. I'm not exactly going with the program. You guys are no closer to opening the veil than you were before—

Not true, Sssamantha. As they say, where there is a will, there is a way. True, you were and are our best option. And, yes, your daughter was and is a viable option, too. So, too, is your sister, both of whom have been witches in past lives, too, although not quite as powerful. But we are looking into other options, Sssamantha. I have no desire to leave you just yet. Although my existence is not enviable, you have proven to be entertaining.

Gee, thanks.

Hearing about my daughter's and Mary Lou's pasts was news to me, although it made sense. After all, why would I be the only witch in the family?

One thing was clear: the devil had lied to my daughter and tricked her into making a deal with him. How binding that was, I didn't know.

It is only as binding as she allows it, Sam. The devil has no real power over anyone.

Unless he possesses them.

Yesss.

A thought occurred to me: *Do you know how to stop the devil?*

There are rumors, Moon Dance.

What rumors?

There is one who knows more than me.

Who?

My son.

6.

Allison was still on babysitting duty.

In fact, per my request, she had taken my kids to go see the latest Marvel movie about some giant bug man. Or was it a mountain lion man? Either way, it gave me some time to work with—and peace of mind, too, knowing they were with Allison, who was proving to be a helluva babysitter. Whether she wanted to or not.

The devil claimed that the dark masters had targeted me, and I decided to ask the dark masters themselves. No, not Danny, who would have been considered a peon. The truth was, he wouldn't know anything, especially considering he never left Anthony's side... 1or his mind. Doing so would, of course, expose him to the devil. No, I knew of one dark master who was very, very high up in the chain of command. A dark master who had positioned herself nicely for a future takeover of the world itself. That is, if I ever gave her the time of day to do so, which I didn't. But to speak to Elizabeth meant letting her out, and letting her out meant potential trouble for me. After all, what if she came all the way out?

I shuddered just thinking about it.

No, I had another source, which was why I was now on the elevator up to the third floor of the Cal State Fullerton Library, which just might have been the biggest library I'd ever seen; then again, I was pretty sure this was the only university library I'd seen. Hell, maybe they were all this big.

The door dinged and I stepped out into a world of books, rows and rows of books. Long rows, too, with high shelves that needed ladders. Here and there, students with earbuds were studying. How earbuds helped studying, I hadn't a clue. I seriously suspected that kids' brains these days were wired differently than my generation. As in, maybe they were born with an auxiliary input just behind their ears.

Officially, the library's Occult Reading

Room didn't exist; that is, unless you happened to have a reason for finding it. I suspected it was the Alchemist himself who determined who had reason enough to find it.

At the far end of the main aisle, I came upon one hell of a long-ass wall. There were no doors along this wall, or windows. Nor were there any desks. I wondered if Maximus had somehow had a hand in that. Indeed, it wouldn't do to have a row of students studying here while alchemists, occult researchers, wizards, witches, and one spunky vampire disappeared through a secret door.

Anyway, I hung a left and headed down the empty corridor, a long row of books to my left. I wondered which row of books paralleled the Occult Reading Room, and saw that they appeared to be anthropological studies of mostly long-lost cultures and tribes. Books about customs and war and even a whole row about hallucinogenic drugs. I looked closer at a few titles. *Shamans and Dream Gates* was the title of one. *The Hallucinogenic Path into Other Worlds - The Shaman's Role* was another. There were more, and each more seductive than the last. Truth be known, most seemed like they belonged in the Occult Reading Room, but, upon closer inspection, they were all written by real field anthropologists, scholars and professors. Most were focused more on the culture, and less on the dream worlds themselves.

Still, it got me thinking about other worlds. I knew the dark masters had been banished to their own parallel world, called the Void. A bleak world, I suspected. After all, why were they so desperate to return to Earth? Well, I knew the answer to some of that. According to Elizabeth, Earth was to be their launching point to conquer the empty spaces of the universe, those vast unknown places that even God had yet to explore, to claim them for their own. I knew Talos lived in his own world, one that was fully realized and beautiful. And just yesterday, I had stepped foot into such a world. Hell, I'd even battled a dragon.

Other worlds. Yes, the words tugged at me, but I let them go for now.

Further down, the nondescript door appeared magically next to me. Unfortunately, a student also appeared at the far end of the hall, hefting a backpack that would undoubtedly give him back problems later in life. I paused in front of some books and projected my inner radar out as far as it would go. A moment later, and there he was in my mind, glancing at books, and when he stood on his tiptoes, scanning a row of books on the shelf above him, I moved swiftly, opening the secret door and slipping inside.

I had just barely closed the door behind me when I heard sneakers running and squeaking from down the hall. The same kid with the backpack appeared very near the door, scanning and searching, his face white. Oops, on second thought, I might not have slipped away as fast as I thought. No doubt the little nerd had turned and caught sight of a foot or buttocks disappearing through the wall.

Now, as he scanned the wall, I watched him through a window that only I could see. He wore broken glasses and a Wonder Woman T-shirt. I might just be looking at the King Nerd. He rapped on the wall, knocking and listening. Now, he put both hands on the wall and pushed. A little, geeky vein popped out on his forehead. I watched all of this with some amusement, and let him believe, even for just a few seconds longer, that magic was real, which it was. But before he could post a video to whatever nerdy channel he ran, I gave him a suggestion to let it all go, that he had seen nothing, that he, in fact, could not remember why he was looking at this wall. That he, in fact, had to go to the bathroom, and badly. The sense of wonder left his face, to be replaced by a pinched look. He did a little dance, crossed his legs, then took off running.

I felt sorry for him, truthfully. He had seen

what he had thought was something extraordinary—and he had. Something out of this world. Something magical and not understood. I pondered for a beat or two, then called him back, with a suggestion that he'd heard someone call his name. And now, there he was, frowning and looking around, and still crossing his legs.

I decided I couldn't destroy someone's sense of wonder, and so I dug into my pocket and found what I was looking for. When he was looking away, I cracked open the door open and flipped a penny into the air. The door was closed well before it landed, and I watched him leap back in surprise when it landed with a metallic clang, the sound amplified in the dead-quiet library. Oops, he might have peed himself. Anyway, he reached down and picked up the coin, examined it, looked around, and assumed it had been tossed from the other side of the bookcase. He pushed aside some books, only to discover the bookcases here were solid, and then he took off running, no doubt to look for whoever had tossed the penny... and for a bathroom.

"Very well done, Samantha Moon," said a voice from behind me, a voice I knew well.

"I'm not sure why I did it."

"Because you understand that what makes

this world interesting—perhaps even fun—is the unknown. You have renewed that primitive part of him that believes in things that go bump in the night."

"But is that so important?"

"The seeking of answers is important, Sam, even if the answers themselves are far less interesting. Once science proves or disproves Bigfoot, most of the fun in wondering will be lost. But it is the search that is fun. That, Sam, is where real living, and a secret to life."

"Is Bigfoot real?"

"Of course. He has long since reveled in his role as the wild man, the very embodiment of which humans seek, to be completely free."

"He wasn't real before?"

"No, Sam. He has been summoned into existence from sheer belief. But let me tell you, he is happy to be here. The wild man loves his role, and basks in it, as you might expect."

We moved to his help desk, which I always thought was kind of cute, especially since I had never seen him help anyone other than me. But there it was, complete with a plaque that read Help Desk, similar to other such plaques in this library.

I said, "Well, I'm here about another creature summoned into existence."

"The devil," he said.

"Gee," I said. "It's almost as if you've read my mind."

***

"I see that your angel, Ishmael, had told you that the devil is only as powerful as you allow. And I see that the one and only Dracula also warned you. Correction, it was Cornelius—the entity within Dracula."

"He's a real peach," I said.

"He was, perhaps, our greatest adversary. At the time, I was too young and too new at the alchemy game to have taken him down. Indeed, Cornelius alone, along with my mother, killed dozens, if not hundreds, of light workers."

"They belong together," I said. "Except they will never be together. Not under my watch."

"Nor mine, Sam. Speaking of which, I see my mother has suggested that a deal with the devil is only as binding as one allows. She speaks the truth. The problem with her statement is that the devil, once inside you, can convince you to allow it. The devil, in essence, can override one's defenses."

"You're not helping me feel better," I said.

"No, I imagine not. Then again, you are not here to feel better, are you, Sam?"

"No," I said. "I'm here to figure out how to

stop the devil."

"And by stop, do you mean kill?"

"If that's what I have to do," I said. "Then again, who am I?"

"Who are you indeed, Sam?"

I was about to ask what the hell that meant, when he went on. "The devil and I have crossed paths many times. You see, he sought out the realm from which the dark masters had been banished, and thought I might give him what he needed. He tempted me as well, and tried to lure me into a particularly clever trap. It was only with the help of other Light Warriors that I was able to untangle myself from his carefully laid plans. He is not happy about it. I do not care if he is happy or not, quite frankly."

I waited, knowing the five-hundred-year-old Alchemist, who just so happened to look like your everyday college student, was going somewhere with this.

"I am, Sam. The devil is indeed alive today because of expectation, because of belief, and because of fear. It was a perfect mix to bring him forth from the ether. But belief has reached a tipping point."

"Tipping point?" I asked. "As in, belief in his existence is sliding?"

The Alchemist nodded. "And rapidly, too. The tide is turning. There are whole generations who do not believe in him or hell or even the afterlife. He feels it, and, I believe, it is weakening him. Indeed, I feel he has made a concerted effort to increase his wicked ways, to wreak even more mayhem and destruction. To remind the world that the devil is alive and well and to be feared."

"Because belief and fear—"

"Keep him strong. Keep him relevant. Keep him alive."

"Not to sound narcissistic as hell, but where do I fit into all of this?"

"I'm not sure yet, Sam. But I see you there, in the mix." He opened his mouth to speak, closed it again.

"See me how?" I asked. "What do you mean?"

"I've been having my dreams, Sam. Prophetic dreams."

"Go on," I said.

"In them, you are connected to the devil's demise. At least, in one version."

"And in the other?"

"You, and everything you love, has been wiped off the face of the Earth."

"Jesus."

"Sadly, He is not in my dreams."

I digested this, then asked, "And how accurate are your prophetic dreams?"

"They always come to pass."

"But they're a little vague," I said. "Either the devil or I die."

"True, Sam. But the key point here is that you and the devil will cross paths, and you will do so in a grand way."

"Whatever it takes," I said, "for him to leave my kids alone."

"Admirable, Sam. But let me ask you: if he knows that your kids are your trigger point, why, then, has he come after them?"

"I don't know," I said. "He needs them?"

"The devil doesn't them, Sam. He has done fine for millenniums without them."

"I-I don't know," I said.

"Think, Sam."

I shrugged. "To cause a reaction in me?"

"Sam, are you aware that the devil is bound by certain universal laws?"

"Sorta."

"One of which states that he cannot strike a human first. He needs to either be invited in, or act in self-defense."

"And who upholds these laws?"

"The ways of the devil, his role in the universe, the laws that govern him, if any, are mostly unknown. Evidence suggests that he shows restraint, for reasons I do not understand, but which point to an agreement with higher beings."

"Fine," I said. "So, what are you getting at? The devil is coaxing me into a fight?"

The Librarian held my gaze, and I suspected I had hit the nail on the head. He said, "Sam, are you aware that there has been a renewed wellspring of prayers—"

"Prayers?" I said.

"Yes, Sam, prayers."

"And you know this how?"

"I am very close to my own guardian angel, Sam."

"And angels are aware of prayers?"

"They have access to them, yes. This shouldn't surprise you. Many of the higher beings in the non-physical realms have access to our prayers. More accurately, they can see our wants and desires, which flash across the cosmos. Our desires are eventually answered, if one believes and allows."

"Am I flashing now?"

"Oh, yes. Sam. Your desire to protect your children is, undoubtedly, shining bright and clear."

"But I didn't make an official prayer."

"Official prayers are not necessary, Sam. Desires spring forth automatically, flashing through the heavens."

"Did you just say, 'spring forth'?"

"I did. I'm showing my age, aren't I?"

"Yes. Go on."

"Your request for the safety of your children has within it a not-so-hidden condition. A condition to defeat the devil."

"So, what are you saying? That my prayer or desires have been answered?"

"Yes and no, Sam. I am saying that the machinations have been assembled for you to do so."

"And you know this, how?"

"I know the laws of the Universe, Sam. And yours is a powerful desire. Powerful desires are heard loud and clear. But first, do you know the purpose of forest fires?"

7.

I blinked. "Forest fires have a purpose?"

"Of course," he said. "This way."

He stepped out from behind the help desk and headed over to the many rows of creepy-ass books. I kept my distance, mostly because I couldn't stand the dark whispering and cries. How he ignored them, I didn't know. He studied the high shelves. For a secret library filled with some of the most dangerous books, pamphlets, and grimoires, it was surprisingly well-lit. I looked up and up, and saw no actual source of light, neither bulb nor halogen. The light just seemed to emanate from somewhere.

"Eternal light from there is all, of all, in all,

Sam," he said, still studying the shelves.

"Um, sure."

"God light. Found originally in the Great Pyramid, it has been passed on for centuries. A similar light burns in the Vatican, another in a secret room beneath the White House, still another in a chamber beneath the Wailing Wall, not to mention a number of Buddhist temples, hidden caves and underground chambers the world over, all of which you are not privy to. At least, not yet. Ah, here we go."

He selected a particularly large book from an upper shelf, using a footstool that just might have hovered up and down on its own volition. He returned to the help desk, and I followed while keeping an eye on the footstool.

"Back to the forest fire analogy," he said as he laid the book before me, not yet opening it. Try as I might, I couldn't read the title upside down, until I realized it was in Latin. I think. He went on, "Forests can be overburdened with fallen trees, hindering the growth of new trees."

"Which is where forest fires come in."

"Indeed, Sam. Fires are a marvelous thing. They cleanse the land and give it a chance to start anew. With one lightning strike, a fire can ignite. With one lightning strike, the burden upon the forest can be eliminated and give room for new life to grow."

"But killing the living, too."

"A sacrifice nature is willing to make."

"I assume the devil is the fire?"

"No, Sam. The devil is the rotting, dead trees that clog the forest floor, the fallen trees that stifle new growth and burden humanity. The devil is the result of tired, outdated fears." Archibald Maximus paused. "You, Samantha Moon, are the lightning strike."

Max opened the book.

8.

"Tell me, Sam, what do you know of the Angel of Death?"

I shrugged. "Dark robe. Hoodie. Carries a scythe. The silent type."

"That's Death, Sam," said Max, carefully turning pages filled with drawings of all types of creatures. Granted, they were all upside down, but I was pretty sure I spotted a dragon, a harpy, humanoids with animal legs. Animals with human legs. Angels, giant men, tiny men, and everything in between. "Some cultures confuse the two. The truth is, one exists and one doesn't. At least, not anymore."

"Death is dead?"

"He is, Sam."

"Are you smoking the funny weed, Maxie?"

"I am not, and please do not call me Maxie."

"What about Archie?"

"I do not see myself as an Archie."

"Neither do I."

"Can we move on, Sam?"

"Sure," I said. "So, Death existed at one time."

"He did, yes."

"Let me guess. People lost their belief in him, too?"

"They did, Sam."

"And he just... died?"

"Yes and no. It is safer to say he was... returned."

"Returned?" I said. "Returned to where?"

"To the Creator. To the light."

"And who returned him?" But then, I caught on. "The Angel of Death."

"Yes, Sam. The Angel of Death has been given the burden to remove those who are no longer necessary."

"And his job is to kill people? Like a celestial hitman?"

"In short, yes. Ah, here it is."

Max spun the book around for me to see. I saw an illustration of a winged angel. A beautiful winged angel, I might add. An angel who seemed to be hovering high above what appeared to be a temple of some sort, complete with massive marble columns. The angel seemed to be emitting a golden light.

"Doesn't look like death."

"I agree."

The pen-and-ink drawing, with just a hint of color, seemed to have sprung from the hand of Leonardo himself, so accurate was it in its anatomical detail. And then, I saw something else. Something I couldn't unsee.

"It just moved."

"Did it now?"

I leaned down a little closer, inches from the beautiful drawing of the beautiful man whose massive, outstretched wings could have spanned a four-lane highway. The thing was, well, the wings flapped ever so slightly. And his hair— sweet mama—his hair had just lifted and fell, too. It was as if a drawing of Fabio had come to life.

"In a way, it had, Sam," said Max, reading my thoughts. "This is *The Book of All Known Beings*. Images contained within are updated in real time."

"What exactly does that mean?"

"It means that these images are an accurate and current depiction of the entity."

"Wouldn't a photograph be easier?"

"Some entities can't be photographed, Sam, as you well know."

"Then who drew these entities?"

"A number of artists throughout time, from Leonardo da Vinci to Picasso to Jean-Michel Basquiat. All contribute from the grave, of course, updating their pieces as needed."

"From the grave?"

"Have a look here."

I looked, confused as hell. And then, I saw it. The book, ever so slightly, seemed to swell in size, as if new pages had been added. A moment later, it shrank again, the book clearly slimmer. It did this, continuously, over and over.

"What am I seeing here, Max?" I asked.

"You are looking at the addition of more beings, and the removal of others."

"Some entities are dying?"

"Indeed, and some are being created."

"As we stand here?"

"Yes, Sam."

"How the hell are they being added to the book?"

"The book you see before you, Sam, is merely a representation of the real book. Think of it as a living copy."

"My brain hurts."

"I imagine so."

"The artists. They were all Light Warriors?" I tried to imagine the edgy Brooklyn street artist, Basquiat, as an Alchemist. Then shrugged. Why the hell not?

"He died too young," Max said, reading my mind again. "But, yes, many of his paintings contain within them coded messages; in fact, all of our artists were adept at hiding secret messages that reached other Light Warriors without giving up our secrets, or our locations, or our lives."

I pointed to the winged angel. "Who drew this one?"

"A master from a bygone era, Sam."

"You don't know?" I asked.

"Unfortunately not. He would have been before my time, and even my own master's time."

"Hermes?"

"Yes."

The Angel of Death shifted ever so lightly, his robes billowing, his sword catching more of the light, gleaming brighter.

"Max, why are you showing me the Angel of Death?"

"Because only he—Azrael—can help kill the devil, Sam."

"But I thought you said my destiny was intertwined with the devil and all that."

"It is, Sam. But I suspect you are going to need a little help."

I tapped the picture. "Any suggestions on where to find him?"

Max shook his head. "Sadly, I haven't a clue. But he is real, I know that much."

"Otherwise, he wouldn't be in *The Book of All Known Beings*."

"In a word, yes."

"This temple with the pillars. Any idea where that's located?"

"I don't, Sam. I'm sorry."

"Well, fat lot of good you've been, Mr. Maximus."

He gave me a small smile. "I apologize, Sam. You'll discover that most creatures in this book are rather difficult to find, let alone archangels."

I tapped the page opposite the Angel of Death. "Like this guy," I said, who looked nothing more than an amorphous shadow, although I could vaguely make out it was humanoid. In fact, I thought I was just able to make out two massive wings.

"Ah, yes. Death's Shadow. At least, that's how I think of him."

"You don't know?"

"The page appeared not too long ago. There's no description."

"Why not?" I asked.

"The creature, you'll note, has not fully formed."

"Then how do you know he's called Death's Shadow?"

"I don't. But if you'll look, they appear as exact opposites."

He was right about that, only the shadow was without shape. "Maybe that's just how it looks."

"No, Sam. It's been taking shape over the years."

"When did it first appear?"

"Within the past decade, I would say."

I watched the misty shadow shift and move, form and reform, all very slowly. He, too, appeared to be sporting a shadowy sword, but it was hard to tell. It could have been a hockey stick for all I knew. And the wings... they could have been something else too.

No, I thought, *they're wings. And they're massive. Nearly as massive as the Angel of Death's own wings.*

"Another thing. Entities aligned or connected are always found grouped together in this book."

"So, he really is Azrael's shadow," I said.

Archibald Maximus nodded, and I thought about that as I continued studying the shadowy

being, feeling oddly intrigued by it.
    And terrified, too.

9.

We were all at Kingsley's manor, where we'd been for the past three days. Kingsley had insisted, and I had agreed. There was, after all, safety in numbers.

With that said, the massive estate was feeling a bit like a frat house, which I didn't mind so much. Truthfully, I did feel safer surrounded by Kingsley and his massive manservants, each of whom just so happened to be variations on the Frankenstein monsters. In this case, the Lichtenstein monsters. Luckily, there was more than enough room for all of us. As an added treat, Allison came by nightly and sometimes stayed over too. I think she enjoyed being around all this masculine energy, even if some of the energy had literally been dead and buried.

"I heard that, Sam," came her voice from the kitchen. "And no."

"Love you," I said, raising my voice.

"You'd better."

"What did she hear?" asked Kingsley above me, since I just so happened to be snuggled deep in his arms.

"There was a small chance that I might have insulted Allison."

"You tend to do that a lot."

"What can I say? It's how I show love."

He thought about that. "So, every time you call me a big lug, what you are really saying you love me?"

"Sure," I said. "Let's go with that."

We were in Kingsley's family room, which was big enough to move into. Kingsley and I were snuggled on one end of the U-shaped couch watching Anthony play on the Xbox. Tammy was seated opposite us, apparently texting her life story, judging from the way her fingers flew over her phone keypad for the past half hour.

Without looking up, she stuck out her tongue at me and continued texting.

In the background, lumbering and limping,

although some were surprisingly fleet of foot, were the Lichtenstein monsters. They prowled Kingsley's spacious home, cleaning, cooking, or just wandering. It would have been creepy if I wasn't used to it—

Never mind. It was still creepy, although my kids didn't so much as blink an eye when one of these things appeared in the room, or when they bowed and tried to smile, or when they picked up our empty dishes.

It's creepy, Sam, came Allison's thoughts.

I nodded. *Thought so.*

But not to my kids, who had more or less grown up with the strange and weird, even if the strange and weird had been primarily me. To my kids, these lumbering, hulking, scarred and misshapen monsters—who were stronger than even Kingsley—were just an everyday, run-of-the-mill norm.

One such creature—a particularly tall fellow with one side of his head missing—accidentally kicked the coffee table. He apologized and reached down to position it back, and dropped the dishes he'd been holding. Most clattered onto the mohair rug. A knife and fork rattled on the glass tabletop.

He apologized, or tried to, his voice so deep as to be nearly incomprehensible. I had just made out the words "sorry" and "idiot" when

Kingsley shot up from the couch to assist him. The creature bowed and apologized and seemed to be close to weeping, when Kingsley pulled him in close and held the back of the man's head in a deep hug. I heard Kingsley reassure the man-thing, telling him he was doing a good job and that he was Kingsley's favorite. He said this to all of the Lichtenstein monsters in private: they were each his favorite. I thought that was kind of cute, and not weird at all.

The creature nodded and tried to smile, but I knew the nerves in his face had been long since destroyed, perhaps when his head had been damaged. Dr. Lichtenstein, his creator, had been a true mad scientist. Not content with leaving well enough alone, the doctor had rearranged body parts, too, presumably to find the best matches. Not all had gone according to plan. Some body parts worked well with some of them, with others, not so much. Some spirits remained attached to the various parts; indeed, one monster might have a half-dozen such entities within him, all crowding for air time. Of course, it was the dark master within each of them who actually fueled the dead bodies. Dark masters, it seemed, cared little for which body they inhabited, as long as they got a body. With that said, many of the Lichtenstein monsters contained low-level dark masters. Lower, even, than Danny.

Most interesting was the bonding that occurred between Kingsley and the monsters. Initially, they had all bonded with Lichtenstein himself; that was, until he found himself stranded in a world far, far away. He could just stay there for all eternity, for all I cared.

Earlier, Kingsley had barbecued some hamburgers for us. Allison, Tammy and I had watched in stunned disbelief as the two boys—Kingsley and my son—had eaten what was surely the equivalent of a full-grown wild boar. I hadn't even finished my chicken breast. Thanks to a magic ring, I could eat, but food still tasted bland. Not terrible, mind you, just not very exciting. Still, just the act of ingesting food with friends and family on Kingsley's spacious outdoor deck—a deck that looked out onto the Carbon Canyon woods, woods which proved to be fertile hunting grounds for Franklin each month.

Anyway, we had been lavishly served by Kingsley's massive—and heavily stitched—staff, a staff fit for a king, surely. It wasn't terrible having our every whim catered to, even if the staff did smell slightly dead. Granted, it wasn't a smell I entirely minded, even though I often watched Allison fight back the vomit. Tammy, too, for that matter.

Afterward, we had all gone for a small walk around Kingsley's property. Yes, the rich bastard had a hiking trail around his property, complete with mileposts. It was precisely three miles around his yard. I noted the high walls, all outfitted with not just barbed wire, but deadly-looking wall spikes, each of which could have been found atop a Crusader's spear. I wondered what his neighbors thought. Then again, his closest neighbor was a mile away. Probably a good thing.

Now we were all in the family room, waiting on Allison's signature coffee-bean crème brûlée. And waiting. You'd think a witch would be faster in a kitchen.

Wait for it...

"That's because I'm not a kitchen witch," said Allison, stepping through the arched doorway, holding a silver platter containing a half-dozen dishes. "And you know that, Sam."

I did, of course. Kitchen witches relied on complicated spells and bizarre ingredients, such as eye of newt and all that. Although effective, Allison was a bit more bad-ass than that—although she was quick to remind me that a kitchen witch could make one's life a living hell, too. Or enhance it beautifully. Spells, after all, worked both ways. Of course, knowing all of this didn't stop my jabs, barbs and digs, all of which entertained me to no end.

"You're impossible, Sam," she said, and began handing out the caramelized desserts, along with little spoons.

Kingsley held his delicately with his paw-like hand and had me giggling in no time. Same with Tammy and Allison. Anthony, not so much. He kept his head in the game and ignored her dessert. Kingsley hammed it up, a true showboat, sticking out his sausage-like pinky. We laughed some more, and when I looked back at Anthony, his dessert was gone. Just like that.

"Any more?" he asked over his shoulder, still smacking his lips, still playing his video game.

"Anthony..." I began, since Allison had just sat down next to me.

"No, it's okay, Sam," she said, getting up again. "I have like a dozen more."

"Bring me four! No, five. Six!"

"And I'll have the rest," said Kingsley, his voice deep enough to make my eardrum tickle. "That is, if everyone is okay with that?"

I had taken, precisely, two bites of my own dessert. Tammy had just dug into hers. And Anthony and Kingsley were already divvying up the rest. Yup, just another night with the gang.

As I ate, and while Allison was busy handing out the rest of the desserts, my daughter shot me the occasional look. She had, of course, long since read my mind—and had long since known—that, more than likely, she had been duped into making a deal with the devil. I had tried to talk to her about it, but she wasn't in the mood. And she might never be in the mood.

But to get to her, the devil had to get through us, and that just wasn't going to happen. Not on my watch, Allison's watch or Kingsley's watch. Or all his hulking, patchwork monsters' watch.

Indeed, there was strength in numbers, but when dealing with the devil, anything was possible. I suspected there was also a very good chance that the devil let us think we were safe. Surely, he had not brought his full arsenal of demons to Santa Ana that night.

So far, the devil had stayed away, and I was beginning to think that this was all one bad dream. How could the devil be connected with me? And was he really using my kids to get to me, to incite a reaction? A few days ago, it had all seemed plausible, so much so that Kingsley had taken us all in. Now, three days later, I felt a bit silly. After all, why would the devil have an interest in me? Who was I to him? I was just a mom with a hankering for blood.

"You're more than that, Mom," said Tammy suddenly, standing. She took up her crème brûlée, with all its fancy accent marks and macrons, and headed out of the family room. She sidestepped a Lichtenstein monster who had been waiting patiently to collect our empty dishes. He nodded as she passed. She ignored him.

"Excuse me," I said to the room, and Kingsley nodded at me. Allie, who had been following my thoughts, made to stand, but I gestured for her to stay. I needed to speak to Tammy alone. It was time.

She was just starting up the curved stairway that led to the bedrooms upstairs when I stepped into Kingsley's massive open foyer which featured an antique table with a Ming Dynasty vase in the center of it, a vase that he'd paid far too much for. High above was a crystal chandelier. I was pretty sure most of my house would fit in his foyer, too.

"I want to be alone," Tammy shouted behind her as she continued up the stairs.

"I heard you say 'alone,'" I said, starting up the stairs behind her. "But what I really hear is: 'Mom, I want to talk.'"

"Oooh, you're impossible!" she shouted to me from the top of the stairs, then marched away, her little hands balled into fists.

She was just about to slam one of Kingsley's oversized guest bedroom doors with its crystal doorknobs when I stopped it. "I didn't raise a daughter would slam a door in her mother's face, and so, I will assume that you forgot just how fleet of foot I am."

She spun around. "Fleet of foot? What are you talking about?"

"It means fast. Like a fox." I slipped inside and shut the door behind me.

"There's nothing to talk about. You can just leave. And there's crème brûlée on your chin."

"I'm leaving it there until you talk to me, young lady."

She had long since stuck out her lower lip, as she'd been doing since she was a little girl. But now, that lower lip quivered, then broke into a laugh. "You look ridiculous, Mom."

I made a show of trying to find the pudding, but kept barely missing it.

"It's right here, Mom," she said, pointing.

I swiped again. "Did I get it?"

"No. And you are doing that on purpose."

My next swipe came away with a dab of crème brûlée. "C'mon, baby. Let's sit down and talk."

"Do we have to?"

"Yes."

Kingsley's guest room she chose was simple: a bed, a reading chair, a lamp, a dresser. Nothing too fancy; same with his other eight guest rooms. Yes, eight. We sat on the edge of her bed. A shadow shifted to slip just behind the dresser. It was, I was certain, a long-dead ghost swinging by, but it was so formless and lost that it might as well have been a living shadow. Then again, it could have been one of the devil's minions.

"Thanks, Mom. As if I wasn't already having a hard enough time sleeping."

"I'm sorry, sweetie. Have I told you lately how brave you were to try to help me?"

"Like a million times."

"Well, you are. And you did your best to try to help me. You couldn't have known that it was a—"

"Trap? Of course, I thought it was a trap. I just thought there was a chance... that maybe he was telling the truth... and that..."

She broke down, weeping into her hands, sobbing harder than maybe I'd ever seen her sob before. I pulled her into me and held her, and let my own tears flow, and, as she cried, she tried to speak, and, dammit, I understood every word. Every blubbering word:

"I can't... I wouldn't know... I can't lose you. I just can't. You're my mommy... my friend... we lost Daddy... but yeah, yeah inside Anthony... not the same... Anthony has really bad BO, like really bad... not normal... I wouldn't know how to... I just don't want... can't lose you. Ever. No. Never..."

She cried some more, and I found her hot tears and breath oddly comforting, maybe even reassuring. I held her tight, and she might have even held me tighter, and when she was finally all cried out, I was certain I heard footsteps just outside the bedroom door. Allison was creeping around again.

"Not creeping," she said from the other side of the door. "Just concerned."

"We've got this covered," I said.

"You sure?"

"I'm sure."

I heard her pad away, then creak down the stairs. Tammy unraveled herself from around my neck, and wiped her nose.

"She's a good friend, Mom."

"I know, baby."

"She'd do anything for you."

"I know."

"Like go to other worlds, fight dragons, and fight demons, too."

"I ask a lot from my friend, eh?"

Tammy smiled and wiped her cheeks, except the tears kept coming.

"What's got you so upset?" I asked.

"The devil wants to kill you, Mommy. I made a big mistake."

I took her hands and dropped to my knees on the floor before her. I looked up at her and said, "I know things look bad, sweetie. And I know there are some very bad people out there who want certain things from us. But I don't plan on going anywhere. Not now, nor ever. And I mean that literally. And no one, but no one, will ever hurt you or Anthony."

"The devil is listening to you, Mommy."

"How?"

"Through me."

"Is he close?"

She nodded again. "He's not very far."

"Close enough that the two of you are connected?"

She closed her eyes, and more tears appeared. "He's inside me, Mommy. And I can't get him out."

She pulled her hands free from mine and buried her face in her palms. "He's laughing, Mommy. Says he owns me. He says he will destroy you and everyone you love. He says no vampire is going to take him down. Not now, nor ever. He's going to enjoy watching you die. He says he's going to use me to kill you."

She wept harder and harder.

My daughter didn't sound possessed. Indeed, she wasn't. There was no fire in her eye, and no deepening of her voice. She and the devil had a mindlink; of course, that, in and of itself, was a terrible, terrible thing for any mother to come to terms with.

"Can you block him, baby?" I asked.

"I-I've tried. He breaks through every time. Except..."

"Except what, baby?"

"There's still a tiny place in my mind that he hasn't found yet. It's like a small box."

"Can you go in there now?" I asked.

"I-I can, but that means..." She searched for words.

"Means what, sweetie?"

"It means I have to sort of shut down. I can't do a lot in there. It's a dark place."

"But safe?"

She nodded, her lower lip trembling.

"Can you go in there now, baby? And maybe sleep?" I asked her. "Sleep all night long?"

She nodded. "I-I think so. The devil says he's gonna find me, though."

I took in some worthless fucking air. "Can you go in there now, baby?"

She nodded, and I watched her eyelids flutter, and then her shoulders sank, and my daughter was nearly a lifeless thing. She breathed and sat straight. The tears stopped and her lower lip quit trembling.

"Are you in there now, sweetie?"

"Yes, Mommy."

"Does the devil know about the Angel of Death?"

She nodded slowly. "Yes, Mommy. He said nothing will help you. Nothing. Not God, not your friends, not Anthony, not your angel, and certainly not Azrael."

I knew the name, thanks to the Librarian. I was just surprised to hear it come from my daughter's lips. The Angel of Death.

"Sleep, baby. You are safe here."

"Okay, Mommy."

As she lay on her side, I pulled the comforter over her.

"Mommy?"

"Yes, darling?"

"Where are you going?"

My daughter, of course, had picked up on my plans. I said, "I'm going to talk to an old friend. A very good friend."

J.R. RAIN

10.

Fang was behind the counter, looking much as I remembered him back in the day, back when he was a bartender at Hero's, my favorite bar where I used to hang out with Mary Lou, back before I had learned that he had stalked the shit out of me.

That was, of course, a long, long time ago. Now, he was one of us: that is, a vampire. And instead of serving just beer and wine, he also served human and animal blood, all done inconspicuously, in clear defiance of any health codes.

He spotted me come through the door and waved me over, smiling broadly. Fang, I noted, still wore his two extracted teeth—his two remarkably long teeth—as pendants around his neck, looking for all the world like two normal-sized shark teeth, rather than two extraordinarily long human canines.

"Moon Dance!" he said, coming around the bar and holding out his hands. Fang was tall and thin, but he was now wiry with muscle. Vampirism had been good to him. He had always been good-looking, but he seemed to have filled out a little over the years since his turning. Indeed, there was a glow to him now, which suggested a recent feeding. Not a big surprise, since he ran a no-kill blood bank. Yes, the many human donors here thought they were donating to a real blood bank. Other than that one ethical hiccup, everything else was on the up and up. In fact, his bar was saving lives by satiating those vampires who might have otherwise killed for their nightly hemoglobin fix. With the faux-donation clinic just next door, I knew Fang had, by now, amassed vats full of human blood, many of which were separated by blood type, racial type, gender type, and even age type. Who knew vampires could be so particular?

The bar itself looked like your typical dive bar. Those two gents in the back, sipping on what looked like red wine, were sipping, of course, blood. Except your average Joe off the street wouldn't know the difference. Fang kept the place dark, kept the music loud. The booths along the walls and window were high-backed, deep and dark, perfect for a vampire who didn't want to draw attention to himself or herself. And for those vampires who chose not to satiate the entity within, or for those preferred to keep the parasite within them weak, or for those who were generally against consuming human blood, Fang also kept on hand some pig and cow blood, ordered from the same damn butchery that I used. Lucky me.

He gave me a big, smothering hug. He even lifted me up off the ground a little. It had been a while since I'd seen him, and the look in his eye was undeniable: the lanky goofball still had it bad for me. Why these men had it for me, I didn't know. But I suspected most women had their fair share of inexplicable crushes. I remember all the crushes on Mary Lou. Boys would literally follow her home daily from middle school and even into high school. Hell, her husband had been one of them.

Of course, my crushes just so happened to be an escaped convict-turned-vampire, a guardian angel, and a big, bad werewolf.

Fang set me down after a half-twirl. "And to what do I owe the pleasure, matey?" he asked.

"I need some help," I said. "And I also need a drink. Not necessarily in that order."

He grinned. "Still animal blood?"

"Still animal. Yourself?"

"Oh, I am into human blood, Sam."

"How's that working out for you?" I asked.

"Edward and I have an agreement."

"Edward?"

"My dark entity. He only comes out to play when I give him permission. And he goes back in when I say so."

"And how's *that* working out for you?"

"Mostly, okay. Lately, I've noticed he tends to stay out longer and longer, even after I call him back."

"That could be a problem," I said.

"I know."

I said, "Cow and pig blood work every time."

"Weakens him?" he asked.

"Yes," I said. Except, I knew Fang might already be too far gone. Meaning... the opening had already been created. His entity, Edward, no doubt had a foothold, which meant he could probably slip out at will. Slip out and take over Fang. I kept that to myself. Fang would discover it for himself. It was a slippery slope consuming human blood; it strengthened a vampire, but also strengthened the entity within.

Fang went over to a row of wine casks, drew from a shiny spigot, and out flowed a thick stream of crimson. When the glass had filled, he turned the spigot, caught a few remaining drops, and set the shimmering goblet of blood before me. Unlike the other vampires who preferred the anonymity of the high-backed booths, I sat at the counter, front and center, not very far from a few mortals drinking their blues away with mugs full of dark beer.

Fang caught me looking at the closest customer, a house painter by the looks of him. Fang said, "Don't worry about Matt. He's a regular, and has long since been given the suggestion to ignore anything and everything vampire- or ghoul-related."

"Ghoul?" I asked.

Fang shrugged. "A good catch-all. I don't know who's going to walk in through those doors."

I raised the glass, tried to ignore the big fat chunk of meat floating in it, and chugged half of it down. Animal or not, the blood hit the spot. Especially my belly, which warmed first, then radiated out in waves. A good feeling. One that also felt lacking. Like drinking a diet soda. Good enough, but missing that sugar kick. The kick, in this case, was the human element.

"So, what's got you down, Moon Dance?"

he asked, leaning his sharp elbows on the bar. It was just like old times.

I considered how much to tell him, then decided to tell him all of it.

***

Fang and I had long since lost our telepathic communication, and so, even I was tired of hearing my voice when I finally concluded with the events of tonight—that is, when I realized the devil had an even deeper connection with my daughter than I had realized.

"His connection is growing, Sam."

"Is it a possession?" I asked.

"Not quite, but close. Enough that he can begin to influence her."

"Well, she's safe for now."

He nodded. "Her locked-up space in her mind will only last so long. The devil—he's going to find a way in."

"He's never going to let her go, is he?"

"At least not until he figures a way to get to you."

"And why doesn't he just kill me now?" I asked. "Send a handful of demons to do the dirty work for him?"

Fang, whose knowledge of the occult was second only to the Alchemist—at least in my experience—shook his head. "It is common knowledge that the devil cannot engage, Sam. Nor can his demons. They can terrorize, yes. They can do everything *but* kill or destroy."

"Unless invited in."

"Indeed, Sam."

"And so, he's what? Scheming, manipulating, orchestrating?"

"All of the above. And, from what you've said, you and the devil are inextricably tied together. But the devil knows the future is not writ in stone."

"Did you just say, 'writ'?"

"I did, Sam. I'm a dork."

Fang was many things, but I had never thought of him as a dork. I laughed and caught his eye. Ah, the fire just behind it was growing. His entity, Edward, was taking an interest in this conversation.

I said, "So the devil hopes to change his fate?"

"It appears so, Sam. And it appears his fate is tied to you."

"Since when did this happen? Why am I the last to know?"

"The future is a strange animal, Sam. Those who see it only see probabilities. Same with prophetic dreams, as you well know. More than likely, the devil knew of his future fate, but had waited until it had seemed more and more likely."

"Like if I had been killed off or something."

"Or, if you had chosen to utilize the diamond medallion."

"His fate is tied in with my vampirism?" I asked.

"More than likely. I cannot imagine how a mortal would take down the devil."

"Well, I can't imagine how I would take down the devil, either," I said. "It's something I've never imagined."

"And yet, you are imagining it now. Funny how this all works."

"But if he had just stayed away..." I began.

"Maybe it was impossible for him to stay away, Sam. Maybe his looking into the Amazing Disappearing Danny Moon led him inevitably to you. And then, his fate, as they say, was sealed."

We were quiet for a heartbeat or two. Which was damn near a full minute.

Finally, I said, "But how do I do it? How do I kill the devil?"

"The Angel of Death, of course," said Fang.

"What do you know about him?" I asked.

"Not much more than Archibald Maximus," said Fang. "Higher immortals, especially those who roam between worlds—and live between worlds—have been created to serve specific purposes."

"Created by who?" I asked.

"A Creator much more powerful than all of us, I suspect."

"But why the need for the Angel of Death?"

"A good question, Sam. I suspect some of these higher creatures don't know how to die, not really. These aren't reincarnated entities. They are one-offs, so to speak. Very powerful one-offs. Also, I suspect, they might be extremely hard to kill."

"Then why kill them at all?" I asked. "Why not leave them be?"

"I think 'kill' is too strong of a word, Sam. 'Return them to the light' is probably closer. And to answer your question, I suspect their end will come when they have completed their purpose here on Earth. Or elsewhere."

"Or if belief in them fades," I said.

"For some entities, Sam. Not all have been created by humankind's common collective. Take the Angel of Death. He would have been created by the Creator himself. Unlike your devil, who was created through mankind's belief and fear."

"He's not my devil," I said. "So, you're saying the devil might have outlived his usefulness?"

"Either that, or belief in him is significantly fading. Or..."

"Or what?"

Fang looked at me. "Or he's gone AWOL. Breaking the cosmic rules."

"You think that's happened?" I asked.

"I don't know, not with certainty. But I suspect he is bending the rules of his creation."

"Rules of his creation?"

"Every creature has rules governing their creation, Sam. Look at humans. They have an acceptable lifespan, an acceptable range of physical and mental abilities, and an acceptable range of spiritual and creation abilities. Sure, there are a few exceptions."

I thought of Charlie Reed and his world of Dur. Boy, were there exceptions!

"But," he continued, "most humans stay within an acceptable range."

"So, the devil has gone outside the acceptable range?"

"Perhaps, Sam. But I also suspect something else is going on. I suspect an exit point was created for the devil."

"And what's an exit point?"

"A known time of death, Sam. We all have them. Many of them, in fact. Most near-death experiences, near-fatal car crashes, near-fatal sicknesses or diseases, were exit points that were diverted through sheer force of will. Through sheer force of life force, too. If a being has decided they've had enough, they will likely succumb, say, to their cancer. If a being decides that, 'Hell no, there's more to live for,' they will likely push through. Upon his creation, there might have been such an exit point built in for the devil as well."

"Well, it looks to me like the bastard *isn't* done living," I said. "He's fighting back like a cornered hellcat."

"Hellcat, indeed. But tell me, maybe he is pushing just to get you to fight back. Maybe you are his only answer to leave this plane of existence. Maybe, just maybe, he's tired of being what he is. Remember the old vamp beneath the Los Angeles River?"

I nodded. I said, "He allowed you to kill him, even though you were just a newbie."

Fang chuckled at that. "He did. And he did it because he was tired of living, Sam. Tired of killing. Tired of drinking blood. Tired of it all."

"And you think the devil is tired of being the devil?"

"I don't know, Sam. But I do know one thing."

"What's that?"

"I miss you."

"I kinda miss you, too."

"Just kinda?"

"Kinda is all I have in me."

He nodded. "Kinda is good enough."

I said, "Tell me more about the Angel of Death."

Fang looked at me, squinted, then said, "Follow me."

11.

"What about your customers?" I asked.

"They're used to me dashing off," he said over his shoulder, as he led me through a side door behind the bar, then through an unused kitchen, down a flight of rickety stairs. He made a right, then another right, then down a long brick-lined hallway, and then finally into an old room that served, I suspected, as his office. Or his vampiric lair. Had I not been what I was, I might have been concerned. This looked like a murder room if I'd ever seen one. Which I had, once or twice.

Except this murder room had an old desk, a chair, a dented filing cabinet and wall-to-wall bookshelves, all packed with books of varying sizes. Not quite as big as the Occult Reading Room, but damn close. It gave off the same creepy vibe. Luckily, though, no whisperings.

Rather than going to his books, Fang opened a middle drawer in his filing cabinet, thumbed through a few manila folders, all while I watched as a half-dozen ghosts flitted through the room, many dressed in clothing from yesteryear. One watched me as I watched him. He seemed to clear his throat, then gave me a deep bow. There were, I noted, a half-dozen bullet wounds—exit wounds—in his back. I bowed as well and he faded away. *My life.*

"Ah, here we go," said Fang. He removed what appeared to be a drawing from a folder. He handed it to me.

"You brought me down here to look at an old drawing of what? A temple?" I asked. In the old picture, a row of Corinthian columns marched down either side of what appeared to be a long, marble hallway. There was a bright light above, which reflected off the marble below. The edges of the drawing were crumbling and the whole thing just looked damned old. If I had to guess, maybe over a hundred years old. A yellowish haze sort of washed out the drawing. Something tugged at me, hard.

"I think it's a temple," he said, "although it's one that I don't recognize."

I didn't either. Then again, I didn't know much about temples. Or anything about temples, for that matter.

"So, why show me?" I asked.

"Such temples are associated with arch-angels."

"Are they now?"

He nodded and proceeded to select a handful of books from his shelves. He flipped through them, and showed me two or three examples. Each depicted a classical archangel within such a temple.

I pointed to the illustration. "How did you get this?"

"Three months ago, a man came in here and gave it to me. He said that I would know who to give this drawing to, and that that the initiate would know how to use it."

"He said, 'initiate'?"

"Yes."

"Did he order a drink?"

"Nope. One minute, I was looking down at the drawing and the next minute—"

"Let me guess," I said. "He was gone."

"Not quite, but he was walking out the front entrance."

I studied the picture, and as I did so, something continued to awaken within me. I had seen these pillars before, but not in the book Fang had just shown me. No, these pillars were situated differently, the hallway longer, too. "What did the guy look like?"

"Short. Balding. White tufts of hair. Long white jacket."

"Vampire?" I asked.

Fang shrugged. "I dropped the ball on that one, Moon Dance. I don't remember if he had an aura or not."

"I'm leaning toward not," I said absently. "So, you just decided to file the drawing away?"

"Seemed nicer than just tossing it out."

"And what made you want to give it to me now?"

Fang's longish face stared at me, unblinking, the fire in his pupil veritably crackling. Finally, he nodded. "You see the light above?"

I did see it, and, yes. Fang, I also noted, suffered from the same long-pointy-fingernail syndrome that I suffered from.

"You said that in the drawing the Librarian showed you, the Angel of Death was high above and looking down into the temple, right?"

"Right."

"I don't know about you," he said, "but that looks like angel light to me."

"Or maybe it's just a drawing," I said.

"Or maybe it's the same place but a different perspective."

I frowned at that. Indeed, this perspective was from the floor looking up into the bright light. But why a picture of the wide-open floor?

"Maybe your own angel might know where this is?" said Fang. "Ishi or something."

"Ishmael," I said, and nearly grinned. Fang had always been jealous of the angel. I said, "And the old guy said that the initiate would know what to do with this drawing?"

"Yes—hey, what's with that look in your eye?"

"I think I know just what to do with the picture," I said.

12.

I told Fang about it, and he didn't like it. Not one bit.

Now, alone in his creepy murder office—well, plus two or three ghosts and me—I summoned the necessary nerves for what I was about to do. Yes, I knew what to do with the picture, and it scared the shit out of me.

I'd done blind teleportation before. I'd teleported to an Alaskan mountain based on a picture, and to the red planet based on another. Not to mention the moon. Turned out, I needed only the image of a landing spot. In the past, I had used photographs. This would be my first time using a drawing.

Crazy, I thought. *Just nuts. Not to mention, it probably wouldn't work.*

It was, after all, just a drawing. Nothing real. I had a brief image of me landing in a music video, like that waitress did in the "Take On Me" video by A-ha. God, I hoped not. Although that singer was damn cute, drawing or not.

I studied the drawing, 99% certain it was the same majestic hall I had seen with Maximus. Except this was from ground level, and contained no archangel, although a light shone from above. It also contained, I was certain, a clear a landing spot for me.

Fang had been very much against this idea of teleporting. Tough shit. It was my choice, and my problem, and he wasn't the one dealing with the devil.

Luckily, he had a bar to run, and didn't stand around trying to talk me out of it for too long, although he had tried. *What if the temple had been demolished?* he had asked. *Or what if it was filled with, say, furniture? Or with people and pews? Hell, what if it was in another dimension? A parallel world?* The last two didn't concern me as much. As I'd proven with my jaunt to the land of Dur, I had learned that I could teleport back easily enough. Not to mention, I didn't need air, and the cold never bothered me anyway. At least, not for the last decade. Yes, I should be fine if it was another world or, as Fang had suggested earlier, between worlds. Whatever that meant. Although his point about the temple being destroyed concerned me. If I teleported into, say, a pile of rubble, I was pretty sure that would be the end of Samantha Moon and her story.

Then why do it? Fang had asked. *Why take the risk?*

A good question, and I had thought about it for a few minutes. The mysterious circumstances of the drawing's arrival intrigued me to no end, although it wasn't enough for me to make such a dangerous jump in and of itself. No, I was willing to risk everything because I was pretty damn sure I would find the Angel of Death there, the one entity who could purportedly help me.

I didn't have time to explain all of this to Fang, not with my daughter locked inside a tiny corner of her mind, doing all she could to resist the entity who had inserted himself into our lives.

All to get to me.

All to flush me out.

Before Fang had left me in his office at my request, he'd said, "Just be careful, Moon Dance. You happen to be one of my favorite people in the world."

I'd smiled at him, and felt what could only be love for him. I'd thought he felt it too, and we had a nice moment—and if his loving face was the last thing I saw in this world, I would take it.

Now that I was alone, it was time to kick the fucking devil out of my life for good. I looked at the old drawing, studied it closely...

And summoned the single flame.

13.

She is in a safe place. She can reach out beyond the room any time she wants, but in doing so, she opens herself up to that which she knows is nearby.

Indeed, even now she can hear it sniffing, searching, scouring her mind.

She is safe here. But she can't do much. Nope. Sleep would be good. She could sleep right here in this corner of her mind, and she could forget that the devil is just outside her door, so to speak, waiting to get in, desperate to get in, hungry to get in.

Her physical body is curled up on her bed, and she can hear the others in the house, hear her brother laughing with Kingsley, hear the heavy-footed monsters lumbering down the hallway, hear Allison talking on her cell phone.

Sleep, she thinks.

Yes, sleep.

And just as she feels herself slipping away, safe in her little room, and safe from the outside world, too, thanks to Kingsley and the monsters —and her own brother, who might be the most bad-ass of them all—she senses the thing stopping just outside the door into her mind.

She hears it sniff.

Then scratch.

She waits for it to move on, but it doesn't.

The devil is here, and he's found her.

14.

I stumbled and nearly tripped.

And when I found my balance, the first thing I heard was my own gasps echoing all around me. And the first thing I saw was a long row of massive Corinthian columns, made from highly polished marble, each topped with beautiful, floral motifs. They continued on as far as the eye could see.

Above was an arched ceiling decorated in what appeared to be stone reliefs that depicted a battle with men on horses, wielding swords and spears and bows and arrows. As far as I could tell, I was alone. Where I was, I didn't know.

But it seemed real enough, as in, not a drawing. And I didn't seem stuck in an 80's music video, either. So far, so good.

A bright luminance appeared high above about halfway down the hallway. In the drawing, the light had been the Archangel Azrael. Here, it seemed to be just that—a light. Either way, like a moth to the flame, I set off in the direction of the light source.

Each footfall echoed a dozen times over in seemingly every direction. Had I been breathing, I was sure my breathing would have been echoing too. As I walked, and as I passed column after column, each more ornate and beautiful than the last, I had the very distinct feeling that I wasn't anywhere on Earth. At least, nowhere that I had heard of or been before. I knew there were beautiful palaces on our planet, some of which were not on display to the general public, but this was unlike anything I had ever seen—or imagined.

It could have been God's house. Like his *real* house. Except there was a very good chance I had met God, and he'd been a homeless man. In fact, the God I had met didn't need this... palace, or whatever this was.

The air seemed different, too. I inhaled, held it, tasted it. It was denser. I could almost taste it. Indeed, it seemed to be a static charge on my tongue.

Nope, I was definitely not in Kansas anymore, nor California, for that matter.

Or even Earth itself.

Just a few days ago, I had taken a similar off-world trip. And not just off-world, but straight into the imagination of another man. A Creator.

No, I thought. It wasn't his imagination. I mean, it had started off as his imagination, but it had come to life with real people, real concerns, real hope and real love... and real fear.

I shook my head at all of it. That had been less than a week ago, and I was still processing it. Now, I was processing this, too.

Yes, the World of Dur had to take a back seat with my concern for my daughter. The devil had locked on to her, dug in deep, and wasn't going anywhere. Not until I forced him to go. I was up for the challenge. I had to be. Indeed, the devil had made it a point to bring the fight home. This was happening, one way or another.

Whatever *this* was.

A fight, I thought. *A fight for my daughter. For me. For all of us.*

I continued walking. Yes, now the air around me genuinely crackled with energy. Interestingly, I saw no spirit activity here, no curious ghosts flitting in and out of existence, no old haunts wandering this way and that. Indeed, the light energy that passed through here, passed through cleanly, unhindered, smooth wave after smooth wave.

The hall was longer than I had thought, too, but at least the light source was getting closer and brighter.

Elizabeth was not happy. She did not like such bright light. I heard her protesting. Hell, I sensed her burrowing deeper into my mind, far away from the light.

But to me, it felt comforting. I think my own soul—which I now knew to be fully contained within me—was reacting positively to the light. I felt a sense of joy, of going home. That this was what heaven might be like. Or as close to heaven as I would get.

It wasn't heaven, of course. I had seen heaven. I had walked its golden streets, even if briefly. No, this place had real air and gravity and density. Heaven had been ethereal. Heaven had been without boundaries, without weight, without effort, or worry.

And I was worried here. Hella worried, as my daughter used to say. I was worried for my daughter. I was worried about the devil. I wasn't too worried about getting back home, but I kind of was, too. I knew I was far from home. Really, really far. And, yes, in the back of my mind, I always worried that the teleportation might not work here. That I might never get home again.

Just a big worrywart.

Mostly, though, I was spellbound. The openness was on par with a major league baseball stadium... that dizzying, vast, wide-open space where men ran around in long johns and slapped each other's asses. This hall had that same ability of making me feel small and insignificant. I was a wandering mote in God's eye, flitting from one column to the next.

The light grew closer still. Mercifully, it wasn't a mirage that kept bobbing in the near distance.

Most definitely not a mirage, because it was also getting so very much brighter, so much so that I could hear Elizabeth whimpering.

There was no denying this light. I almost felt sorry for the pathetic, dark, evil bitch. Almost.

I picked up my pace a little. Not hard to do when I thought of my daughter hiding in her own mind, curled into a tiny ball in her guest room. Now, I was jogging, then running faster. I passed column after column, and still, the light grew brighter and now, warmer.

So warm. And so close.

And then I stopped and shielded my eyes

and felt the glorious warmth radiate from somewhere high above...

15.

He looks up and frowns.

There's not much that can pull Archibald Maximus from one of his deeper meditations, but this does.

He cocks his head a little, wondering what it was that had alerted him, but soon recognizes that it is, in fact, his own intuition, which he has long since come to trust. The question is: why had the image of The Book of All Known Beings *floated into his consciousness?*

He doesn't know, but he has long since learned not to ignore such impulses—or even random-seeming thoughts.

And so, the Alchemist—as he thinks of

himself—rolls to his knees and then smoothly onto his feet. The movement used to be easier, in centuries past. Now he can feel the small pain in his knees, the wobble of his legs. He is feeling his age in this moment. His considerable age. He knows that he has, at best, only a few centuries left, and then, even his incantations won't save him, and he must train another.

An image appears in his thoughts as he walks through the darkened room. The image is of a familiar young man, Anthony Moon. The Alchemist nods to himself. Anthony Moon, yes.

He opens the portal door, waits for the sense of disorientation to pass, and steps out into the hallway. His darkened room would have been considered very far from the Occult Reading Room. Very far indeed.

He moves down the gloomy hallway, and hears the forlorn cries from the adjoining room, the library adjacent. They call to him, beg him, beseech him. They want release. They want help. They want redemption. They want to bargain. Little does Samantha Moon know just how many entities are trapped in these many books. She only hears a small fraction. He hears them all. After all, he is responsible for their imprisonment.

He steps into the small library and the eternal light awaits. Earlier, he had, of course, shown The Book of All Known Beings *to Samantha Moon. Had the vision of the book bubbled up from his subconscious because it had been fresh in his mind? He didn't know. But he didn't think that was it, either. He knew the difference between memory and prescience.*

He finds the book and takes it to a reading table, sits and opens it. He makes short work of flipping through it this time; having done so just hours earlier, he knows exactly where he is going.

Yes, there is Angel of Death, blond hair wavering ever so lightly, ruling over his marble hall. But nothing about this image stands out to him now. He continues scanning the page... until his gaze falls on the page opposite, to the Angel of Death's shadow, the amorphous shadow he had shown Samantha Moon earlier.

Except, of course, it isn't amorphous anymore. Granted, it's not exactly clear either, but he can see a shape coming into focus, a shape coming through...

A shape he knows well.

16.

I wasn't sure what I had been expecting to see—a burning orb, perhaps, a mini-sun, maybe —but I sure as hell wasn't expecting to see a winged man dropping down from above, a winged man who emanated light like the sun.

No, not a man, I thought, shielding my eyes. *Anything but a man.*

Wind rushed around me, blew back my hair and slapped my clothing. Had there been dust to speak of, I was sure it would have gotten in my eyes. The entity hovered a few dozen feet off the ground, his wings as wide as two school buses. Okay, maybe the short buses. They undulated the way a hummingbird's wings might, a bird famous for hovering in space. And now he drifted down, wings at full sail, his body long and muscular, and his torso bare and perfect. He wore loose white trousers tied with a thick cord around his narrow waist. I took in all of this as he settled before me. His wings folded in on themselves—halving smaller and smaller—until they disappeared. I was pretty sure my mouth was hanging open.

He smiled at my amazement. His smile was radiant and perfect. I was reminded of Ishmael, my one-time guardian angel, but this entity was bigger still. Not by much, but definitely by a foot or two.

"If that impressed you," he said, "then have a look at this."

He turned and there upon his bare, muscular back glowed two beautiful and iridescent tattoos of wings. He smiled again at what must have surely been wonder on my face. "Only an illusion. The wings are there, but they are hidden in—how should I say it?—another dimension."

"I..." I began, then closed my mouth, since I didn't know what to say.

"You don't understand. Not surprising. I barely understand the concept myself." He faced me again, and all I could see was his abdomen that rippled up into a muscular, square chest, a chest that wasn't just for show. There was real power there, as well as in his arms, which were surely as big as Kingsley's. No mean feat.

Keeping his eyes on me, and surprisingly, smiling warmly for someone who I assumed was the Angel of Death, he opened his hands before me, wiggled his fingers, then slipped them into something invisible, all the way down to his wrists, all of which disappeared from my view. For all intents and purposes, his hands were gone. But out they came again, along with what appeared to be a tunic. He shook it out, grinned at me again, and then tossed it over his shoulders, his arms smoothly finding the sleeves. And just like that, the muscular, knotted torso was gone. And so was that chest. Mercifully, the tunic's sleeves were short, revealing most of his arms.

"Am I dreaming?" I asked.

"Very few vampires dream, Samantha Moon."

"You know me?"

"Of course. I've been waiting for you. Whether or not you showed up was another story. But here you are."

I opened my mouth to speak, but words failed me.

He smiled. "Although I go by many names, you can call me Azrael."

"The Angel of Death," I said.

He bowed deeply, and his long, golden hair dropped down off his shoulders and hung nearly to the floor. "At your service."

I didn't recall having someone bow so formally to me, and I was taken aback. If I could have blushed, I was sure my cheeks would have been crimson. To hide my embarrassment, I said, "Where are we?"

"My home, of sorts. Truth is, I'm rarely here. There is, after all, too much to do."

"Too many dead to take care of?"

"Yes and no, Samantha. My role as the Angel of Death is a temporary one. I am, first and foremost, an angel."

"An archangel," I said.

He gave me a lopsided grin. "I didn't want to boast, but yes."

"Are all archangels so informal?"

"Most are pretty uptight. Take your one-time guardian angel, Ishmael."

I nodded, agreeing. "He kinda takes himself too seriously."

"There is that," said Azrael. "Truth be known, your angel hasn't been exposed to human interaction. He doesn't know how to act any different."

"But he's been watching over me, he claims, for eons."

"And so he has, from afar. Remember, I am not a guardian angel. I do not keep in the shadows. I am among men, and among the immortals, too."

"And you speak perfect English."

"I speak every language perfectly, Sam. And someday, so will you."

I frowned at that but let it slide. "Can you read my mind?"

"No. Only one's own guardian angel can do that."

I nodded. "So where are we, exactly?"

"We are between worlds, between realities. We are in a place very similar to where your dark masters venture off to when you sleep."

"You know of them?"

"Of course, Sam. Like your devil, I seek them as well."

"Why?"

"Unlike your devil, I do not seek to entrap them in their personal hells. I seek to liberate them into the light."

"Return them to the Creator."

"You know of this?"

"I do," I said.

"Then, yes. It is time for them to go home. And someday, Samantha Moon, it will be time for you to go home, too."

"You will be there to see to it?"

He looked at me with eyes that seemed to soften. "Yes."

"What, exactly, do you do?"

"I escort them, Sam."

"And you will escort me, too?"

"I will, Sam. Someday."

"Back to the Creator?"

"Back to the light."

"Where I will be re-absorbed."

"A not-very-pleasant way of putting it. Where you will come home and be more free than you have ever imagined."

"I like that," I said.

"You will. Do not fear death."

I took in some electrified air, held it in my lungs, then let it out. This conversation had gotten more emotional than I was prepared for. I decided to change the subject. "Do you live alone?"

"Death is a solitary business, Sam."

"You were waiting for me," I said. "Why?"

He looked at me, and some of his jaunty demeanor slipped away, and I saw, perhaps for the first time, the stoic angel he might have once been. "I am not omniscient, but I can see into the future. Not far, but enough to do my job. The real question is, why have you come?"

I opened my mouth to answer, then closed it again. To speak the answer seemed so... presumptuous—and so murderous. It also seemed ludicrous. Then again, I was in a great hall, located somewhere between worlds, talking to the Angel of Death himself. Either that, or I was babbling incoherently in a padded room somewhere, as I secretly suspected, even after all these years.

Stark, raving mad or not, I still had a devil problem, and so I said, "I want to kill the devil, and I want you to show me how."

17.

"An admirable ambition, Sam. Most people use other means to defeat the devil: through prayer, through ritual, through angelic protection. But you seek to not just stop him, but destroy him."

"No, I seek to kill him," I said.

"I see. Few mortals or immortals have ever uttered such words. Most assume he cannot be killed, only cast into a lake of fire. Or destroyed by Jesus. Or by God. No one thinks, nay, assumes, they can do themselves."

"Look," I said. "I just spent the last minute or so questioning my sanity, and you are only confirming I'm a lost cause. I'm nuts, I get it.

I'm as wacko as wacko gets. But that bastard is doing all he can to make my life a living hell and one of us has to go, and I don't plan on it being me. And if it is me, so be it. At least I will have died trying to rid my family of this fucking puke, pardon my language."

"Your reasons are compelling, Samantha Moon. Of that, I have no doubt. There is one hitch in your plan."

"And what's that?"

"The devil is in the middle of an exit window. A small window, granted. But it is here, upon us. He knows and I know it. And now, you know it, too."

"Then what's the hitch?" I asked.

"I can't kill the devil. I am not a warrior. I am a carrier only."

"You only escort the deceased to the light."

"Yes."

"And someone else does the dirty work."

"If you prefer to call it that. In truth, you would be doing the devil a favor."

"You lost me."

"He has chosen this exit point."

"Chosen it, why?" I asked.

"Each and every life is given opportunities to return to the light. He is no different."

"Are you saying the devil wants to die?"

"Maybe, maybe not. For all I know, he very

much wants to live at this point in his existence, and has no plans to die."

"Then why did he pick a fight with me?" I asked. "He could have done nothing, and his exit window would have passed and I would have been none the wiser."

"Funny how fate works. What first led the devil to your doorstep?"

"He was looking for Danny, and we met at a Jamba Juice."

"The devil is not omniscient either, Sam. But he would have recognized his destiny when meeting you."

"He didn't know about me beforehand?"

"An inkling only, Sam. He would have known the time, the place, and a sense of who you were. But upon meeting you, it would have all become abundantly clear."

"Then why not attack me then... wait. I know. Because he couldn't."

"Nor would he have wanted to. The devil enjoys games, and he enjoyed drawing you out. And he will enjoy his final battle, for not even he—nor I, nor anyone—knows the final outcome."

"And he wants to prove that he can kill me."

"Perhaps. Another possible explanation is momentum. He would have known his exit window was opening, was approaching, and he would have been preparing for what he might have thought—and rightly so—was the battle of his life."

"Does the devil actually fight?" I asked. "I've only seen him as a shadowy piece of black tissue paper, flitting from body to body."

"The devil is an unknown quantity. No one has seen him at his full power. Indeed, he's never had to use it."

"He's never fought for his life?"

"No, Sam."

I said, "So, are you helping me or not?"

He threw back his head and laughed, and it was the perfect sound—smooth, rich, deep—even if I didn't know why he was laughing. "I see the Universe has made no mistake with you, although I knew it hadn't."

"What do you mean?"

"It will take fire to beat the devil. And it will take drive. It will take hate, too. But most of all, it will take heart, and of that, you have an abundance."

"Well, I'm glad you are enjoying this," I said. "But that doesn't help me remove the devil from my life."

"No, it doesn't. But this will."

It was in his hands before I could blink. In fact, I was pretty sure it had materialized out of thin air. Or perhaps it had been in that magical pocket of his. Either way, an obsidian sword lay across his palms, black as night, although it was flecked with what appeared to be silver. The weapon pulsated slightly, as if with an inner light, or inner life.

"A sword?" I asked.

"Not just any sword, Sam. The Devil Killer."

***

"Before you accept the sword, Samantha Moon, you need to know a thing or two."

"Don't run in the house with it?"

Azrael looked at me, cocking his head to one side. He was easily three feet taller than me, and as beautiful as they come. I wanted to run my fingers through his golden hair, just to see if it was real. He smiled down at me, and said, "Amusing, but not. First and foremost, the sword cannot be given back or abandoned or lost."

"Say again?"

"The sword is bound to you always, Sam. Forevermore. Should it be lost, you will seek it out until you find it. Should it be stolen, you will be compelled to recover it. And should it be seized in battle, you will have long since died. It is a soul artifact. In essence, it will become an extension of you."

"I really only plan on using it the one time."

"Your plan is misinformed. You are familiar with the term deputizing?"

"I am," I said. That I knew the term from watching *Bonanza* as a kid, I kept to myself.

"Good. In essence, I am deputizing you, Samantha Moon. Except, in this case, it is for all eternity."

I suddenly recalled the amorphous picture opposite the Angel of Death in Max's *Book of All Known Beings*. I also recalled the name under it. "Death's Shadow," I said.

The entity before me lifted and fell, his sandaled feet never really touching the polished marble floor. Hell, maybe mine didn't either. I looked up to his face, and saw that the pleasant and excruciatingly handsome features had darkened, and I suddenly could imagine him taking souls. The Angel of Death was here. A thought popped into my mind. He looked grim and haunted. I sensed he did not enjoy his job, but he did it out of obligation. The Grim Reaper, indeed.

"You have been well-informed. Yes, Death Shadow. An agent of mine. But only if you accept the sword."

"And if I don't?"

"Then it will remain with me until another

comes."

"And the devil will have his way with my family," I said.

"There's always another answer, Sam. The devil is not without vulnerabilities. Nor are any of us."

"But the best answer is the sword," I said.

"It is the final answer."

"But if it's the final answer, why am I bound to it?"

"Because the devil has been busy over the millenniums, Sam. He has saturated the world with his creations. Not all are demons."

"The devil dog," I said, nodding.

"Indeed, Sam. But there are more. And most are powerful beyond reason, fast beyond comprehension. Their claws drip poison, and once unleashed, they kill quickly, violently, and will consume the body completely."

"These aren't your Sunday school demons," I said.

"No. But the good news is: the sword can dispatch them all. Every last one of them. That is, of course, if you get through tonight."

"Of course," I said.

"Now, will you accept the sword, Sam?"

I opened my mouth, closed it again. The room was empty and beautiful and lighted from a source I could not see. Then again, the light just might be coming from Azrael himself, who still shone brightly. He held the sword before him in both hands, one around the handle, and the other just under the flat blade. The sword itself seemed more useful than beautiful. Not too many accessories and attributes. The hand guard was rounded and wide, protecting the hand as it should. The blade itself was pitch black and would have been considered a broadsword, with two edges and serrated near the handle. The only accoutrement was a blood-red gemstone at the pommel. The whole thing seemed longer than I would have been comfortable with.

"And if I take this sword..." I began.

"The moment you touch it, you are bound to it forever, Sam."

"Can I have my own cool secret pouch?"

He gave me a small smile. "Yes, Sam."

"I won't cut myself in, say, the shower?"

"Doubtful."

I considered his words, all of them, knowing that my life was about to forever change. Or end within the next few hours. I said, "I would, in essence, be working for you, then."

"In essence. But think of us more as a team."

"Would I be, you know, an angel, too?"

He shook his head. "You will always be

what you are," he said.

"A better-than-average bowler?"

"A vampire, Samantha."

I thought about that. He probably didn't know about the diamond medallion. No, I didn't always *have* to be a vampire. I had options, limited as they were. Like he said, he wasn't omniscient, and he couldn't read my mind. He probably didn't know about the medallion.

Either way, I held out my hands, and said, "It's a deal."

Azrael nodded that beautiful head of his, stepped forward, and placed the sword in my hands. And as my fingers curled around the hilt and blade, I could scarcely believe that I had gone my whole life without it. I felt complete, whole, perfect. I wanted to cry, but I didn't. But then, I did, a little.

"Now, are you ready to learn the ways of the sword?"

"I've never been more ready in my life."

18.

Much later, I made the leap from one world and into the next.

I aimed for the big, empty space in Kingsley's office, trusting that even he wasn't working this late. I felt bad, having left the bulk of guard duties to my friends, but I felt confident they—and the eight Lichtenstein monsters—could handle themselves. If anything, Kingsley's manor was overly fortified.

Never enough, I thought, especially in light of what I'd learned these past few... hours? I sure hoped it was hours and not days, although I suspected time slowed down in Azrael's palace, although I couldn't be sure.

The good news: there was nobody inside Kingsley's study, and it was laid out just as I remembered, with its big open space between his desk, bar and conference table. Kingsley's home office was nearly a mirror image of his work office, complete with his obsession with moons.

I waited for the stronger-than-normal dizziness to pass, all while tuning in to my own inner alarm. No ping, nothing. Good... wait. There it was... an ever-so-faint blip, just inside my ear. Danger wasn't here. But it was coming.

First things first. I checked on my daughter, cracking open her door, and saw that she was sound asleep. Good. Very, very good. Next thing, I checked on Anthony—but he wasn't in his room. I checked the time on my cell, and noted that AT&T claimed I was still in roaming mode. Boy, had I been roaming! It was nearly midnight.

These kids were going to be the death of me.

From downstairs, I heard a familiar guffaw, and the *thump-thump* on the floor that always followed it. Good, Anthony was downstairs. Now, I heard Kingsley's voice, followed by Allison's. At the far end of the hall, a Lichtenstein monster appeared, bowed slightly, and disappeared into one of the rooms. One arm was distinctly longer than the other. Strange house.

I was about to head down to see the gang—and really looking forward to sinking into Kingsley's arms and trying to forget that I had just spent some time with not one angel, but two angels—when I heard a door open behind me.

"Mommy?"

I turned and saw my teenage daughter's head poking through the door. "I thought you were asleep, baby."

"I had a bad dream," she said, sounding a lot younger than her years.

"I'm sorry, sweetie," I said, coming to her and wrapping an arm around her shoulders. She was ice cold. "Do you want to talk about it?"

"I dreamed about the devil."

"I'm sorry—"

"Except..."

"Yes?"

Her voice lowered, deepened. "Except it was no dream."

I pulled away, keeping her at arms' length, and studied her face. In particular, her eyes. She was smiling—bigger than normal—and now bleeding from where she had bitten her lip. Most disturbing, though, were the twin flames burning in her eyes.

***

By the time I pulled her into her room and shut the door, the twin flames were gone, and so was the creepy smile. Her voice had returned to normal, too.

I spent the next few moments comforting her as she wept hard, telling me over and over that she was sorry, that she was weak, that he had come to her in her sleep, that he had found a way into the little room of her mind, that she wasn't strong enough, that he had scratched and clawed and broken into the little room in her mind.

I told her it wasn't her fault, that she was going to be okay, and as I spoke, her lips twisted back in what looked like pain, baring her teeth. She shook her head, crying out. And then, she stopped shaking, turned her face toward mine, and opened her eyes. The fire was there in each pupil. Not quite as bright as I had seen it in others. But it was there.

"Hello, Samantha Moon," said my daughter, except it wasn't my daughter, of course.

I wanted to freak out. I wanted to call out to Allison and Kingsley. Or call up a local priest. But I knew this was part of the game. As fucking terrible as this was, I knew this was what had to happen. Azrael had warned me about it. It was the dance before the fight. I had to play along, or the devil would do all he could to ruin us, and probably ruin us quickly too.

"Hello, you piece of shit."

My daughter threw back her head and her piercing laughter was something terrible to hear. "You are a feisty little bitch, aren't you?"

"You are about to see how feisty I am."

"Really now?"

"Yes."

And here it was, although it came faster than I'd expected. To engage the devil, Azrael had said, I had to threaten him. I had to release the devil from the bonds that kept him in check. To kill the devil, I had to free the devil, terrible as that sounded.

"Why, Samantha Moon, is that a threat?"

I looked down at my pale hands, which seemed to glow in the light. I was speaking to the devil through my daughter, and I could never, ever imagine a more horrible situation in all my life. But it was forced on me by the bastard himself. I clenched my hands into fists. So tiny, I thought, compared to what I was up against.

"You bet your ass, it's a threat," I said.

"Well, now. That changes everything, doesn't it?"

"I imagine it does."

"Tell me, Samantha Moon. Do you really think you can kill the devil?"

"No, not really," I said. "But I'm going to die trying."

My daughter threw back her head and laughed—sharp and loud. "You understand what you have done, Samantha Moon?"

"I do."

"Then, let the games begin."

At the same time, the fire winked out of her eyes, my inner alarm raged through my head. I dove for my daughter, shielding her with my body, as something blasted through the window —and through the far wall. Something dark and fast. It could have been a missile. But it hadn't been.

No, it had been a demon.

***

"A demon unleashed is a terrible thing, Sam."

"What do you mean by unleashed?"

"Given permission to attack."

"And they receive permission from the devil?"

Azrael nodded. "Despite popular belief, demons are not fallen angels. Demons are true devil spawn."

"He's a Creator, too," I said.

"He's an architect of the rarest kind. Not

only does he create an endless variety of personal hells, he populates them with demons and other nasties. Many of which you will meet tonight."

"Oh, joy."

"No, Sam. There will be no joy tonight. There will be suffering of the highest order."

***

I threw open the door, shouldering away some of the wood that came tumbling down. Grunting, I held the doorway open as Tammy ducked under me and out into the hallway.

Wind thundered through the opening, and I turned back, looking up into the sky through the broken window and the damaged wood around it—and saw black shapes high above, circling against the stars and half-moon. I could have been a deep sea diver looking up at the silhouettes of great white sharks. Except these shapes sported massive wings—and were as black as night. One by one, they peeled off and shot down.

"Go!" I shouted to Tammy. "Downstairs! Hurry!"

***

"It was made with the devil's agreement."

I blinked, staring at the glowing sword. "The one sword that could kill the devil was made with his agreement?"

"It was. In fact, he helped forge it."

"But why?" I asked.

"Even he saw the desirability of exiting his life, Sam. The problem being, of course—"

I felt like I knew the answer to this one and jumped in: "He can't be killed."

"Indeed, Sam. There was no known way to end his life. But he knew, and helped forge this sword. I suspect he regrets doing so."

I marveled again at it in my hand. The blade glowed ever so slightly. I could feel the heat coming off it. "Dare I ask what it's made out of?"

"The finest metals, Sam. But it is not the composition of the sword that can end the devil's life."

"Then what?"

"It is the intent behind it. The agreement of it. The devil understands few humans or mortals could find the sword. Indeed, it was given to me to safeguard, to be given only to one who is—"

"Worthy?" I jumped in.

Azrael smiled. "Determined enough to find me."

"Fine," I said. "Whatever. I've got this," I said, holding up the sword. "Can it kill his demons too?"

"It can end all of his creations, Sam."

"Good to know."

"Now, shall we practice?"

"With you?" I asked.

"No, Sam. I am not a fighter. There is another. A great warrior in his own right. I believe you've heard of him?"

***

An explosion shook the house.

My knees buckled as I ran, and I knew another demon had burst through the walls like a kamikaze fighter pilot—minus the plane, and minus the suicidal intent—but using its body to smash through the house.

Holding Tammy's hand, we had just reached the top of the stairs when Kingsley appeared at the mountain of debris. "*Sam!* Are you all right?"

I nodded, picked up my daughter and threw her over a shoulder. She barely protested when I leaped over the banister and plummeted twenty feet to the polished floor of the wide-open foyer below. I landed on my feet as vampires are wont to do.

"What's happening, Sam?" shouted Kingsley, ducking, as something exploded above us. It sounded as if the roof had been torn free.

Now, a black shape burst through the square glass above Kingsley's front double doors—and obliterated most of the door too. I was not very surprised to see the three-headed devil dog, Cerberus, its heads all snapping and growling. The fire in their eyes blazed, black smoke billowed from their nostrils.

Kingsley turned to me. "Take everyone down below, to my cell. They'll be safe there. Go!"

And with that, my boyfriend of many years contorted his head and dropped to all fours—and burst from his sweats and tank top. I pulled my daughter away before she got a look at Kingsley's own full moon. I took her hand, running and ducking as furious growls erupted seemingly everywhere at once.

I had barely reached the hallway when Franklin appeared, looking ferocious and pissed. He spied the activity behind us, nodded at me once, then dashed forward. Behind him dashed nearly all the other Lichtenstein monsters. I turned back to see monsters, a giant wolf and a three-headed hellhound in a battle to end all battles. I watched one of the heads pick up one of the Lichtenstein monsters, and cleanly bite him in two.

I pulled Tammy along and reached the family room. There were Allison and Anthony. She had her hands around his shoulders. To my amazement, my son didn't look frightened.

"Sam! What's happening?" asked Allison.

"Demons," said Tammy. "And the devil isn't far behind."

I wanted to vomit. "Allison, take the kids downstairs—"

"No way, Mom. I'm helping," said Anthony, tearing himself free from Allison's grasp. His speed was uncanny, and he ran past me before I could even scream his name, which I did.

I turned and ran after him, but stopped when my son plunged through the hallway and out into Kingsley's open foyer with the vaulted ceiling, because something flashed bright enough to stop me in my tracks, nearly as blinding as Azrael himself. When I blinked, my son was gone, and something massive—and fiery—was in place.

"He'll be okay, Mom," said Tammy, tugging on my shoulder. "Hell, I almost feel sorry for the dog."

She was right, of course. I had to believe he would be okay—at least for the next few minutes. Something flashed in the hallway, and I caught sight of a blazing sword. It was followed by a terrible screech and I was certain my son had just mortally wounded the devil dog.

I turned to Allison. "Take Tammy downstairs, and stay there." I noted one of the Lichtenstein monsters holding open the door to the cell. Kingsley must have told him to watch over us as well.

"What about you, Sam?" asked Allison.

"I'm going to help out up here."

"I can help, too!" she said, and her eyes darted over my face. She was scanning my thoughts. No doubt she picked up on what I'd experienced with Azrael—and what I had to do. "Trust me, you are going to need me."

"Okay," I said. I turned to Tammy. "Go with him, young lady. And stay down there until I come for you. You got that?"

She nodded, and I was relieved to see her eyes were fire-free. She ran to the cellar door, located in a nook just off the kitchen, and headed down with the Lichtenstein monster, who closed the door behind them. She, too, should be safe. At least, for the next few minutes.

I had just turned back to Allison, determined to check on my son, when something black and massive exploded through the kitchen window.

19.

A flash of light from above, and I watched as another angel descended, his own beautiful wings outstretched, shining, if possible, even brighter than Azrael, whom he landed next to. I watched in amazement as his own wings folded in on themselves and disappeared into, no doubt, another glowing tattoo.

The angel before me was just as beautiful as Azrael and Ishmael. And, dare I say, even more so?

"Let me introduce you to the Archangel Michael," said Azrael. "Our best warrior."

Michael nodded, and some of his beautiful brown locks fell forward as well. Before me stood two of the most gorgeous creatures in creation, and I was not hating my life; at least, not in this moment.

"Hello, Samantha Moon. Shall we begin?" he asked.

And begin we did. Michael brandished his own glowing sword, and proceeded to put me through the steps of fighting. He taught me basic maneuvers and slightly more advanced ones. Turned out, I was a bit of a natural, even if the sword was awkwardly large for me.

Although the devil and his spawn didn't have flesh-and-blood hearts, I was to strike where their hearts would be, in the chest. As we practiced, and as Azrael watched, I would learn that the devil was a Creator in his own right. He and his creations existed mostly in a parallel place created by the devil himself, a world that was overlaid on top of this one. I would learn that the devil and his minions could wink in and out of existence, moving between worlds. I would learn that demons, once let loose, could strike with real physical force—and would kill with reckless abandon. I would learn the demons would be weaponless, although their long claws were weapon enough.

Archangel Michael, whose movements were perfect and pure and fast, would put me through my paces, and soon, we were moving together in a choreographed fight, my movements nearly as smooth as his, although not quite. Lucky for me, I was a fast learner.

Meanwhile, Elizabeth hid in the shadows, even while my own soul rejoiced. This was, I suspected, the closest to heaven I would ever get again.

***

Glass and wood, and even a flying bar stool or two, exploded around me. Oh, and one nasty demon, too.

I had just dodged a tile from Kingsley's kitchen counter, when three long black spikes followed just behind them. Spikes that were attached to a black arm, itself appearing out of a long black sleeve. I dove to the side, but not fast enough; its claws dug deep, burning grooves into my back. I cried out, tumbling, as a flash of light appeared somewhere behind me. I had a brief glimpse of the demon itself hurtling back through the opening from which it had come.

Gasping, my back burning, I turned to see Allison slumped against the wall, her hand outstretched, a deep cut over her eye. One of the tiles, I suspected, had hit her. Her hand dropped down. Allie was out.

Pain lancing through my back, I had just

started clawing my way back to her when the demon reappeared at the entrance, screeching like a banshee. And, for all I knew, it was a banshee.

I moved away from Allison, keeping the freaky bastard focused on me.

The devil had made a doozy. The thing before me was hooded, but the hood was also a part of it, too. Its head shifted and jerked, like a bird's head—but unlike a bird's head, his appeared both flat and three-dimensional simultaneously. The demon—if that was what this was—towered over me, just missing Kingsley's twelve-foot ceilings. Its body, like its head, formed and reformed before me. Sometimes I saw through it, too. Other times, it was the blackest black I'd ever seen. It seemed, if anything, composed of living smoke. Most telling were the eyes. Leaping, crackling twin flames. Real flames, too. Not the flames I saw behind Tammy's eyes earlier. No, these suckers were burning with a fury, trailing smoke, and leaping out from its face like pilot lights gone amok. The two strange-looking spikes rising above its back were, I knew, its folded-in wings.

I continued moving away from Allison and —thank God—it locked onto me, not my defenseless friend.

It turned, shifted, tracking me—and our little "sizing each other up" party was over. It lunged forward, swiping both claws. I ducked, spun, rolled, and ended up under the little kitchen nook table where Kingsley and I had sat and drank—and watched it get cleaved into thirds by claws that just missed my face. I crab-crawled backward, and found myself pinned against the china cabinet at one end of the kitchen. Three clawed spikes came at my face and there was nowhere to duck or roll toward. My attacker could have been the Wolverine himself, minus the wife-beater tank top, muscles and yummy sideburns. Oh, and minus the laws of physics, too. It moved effortlessly, instantly, and I suspected it was somehow both in this world and another, simultaneously. It was the only way to explain its herky-jerky, mind-bending movements. Now, its claws were before me, slashing, trying to take my head off. I ducked instinctively—everything I did was instinctive. There was no planning, no calcu-lating, not when something was this fast. Glass shattered over me. I was pretty sure my head was where it should be.

I was pinned, which was a terrible place to be, and as its hand rose for another swipe at me, I did the only thing I could think of...

***

I summoned the single flame, and saw within it the open space directly behind the demon.

I felt myself rush toward it just as air passed over me. Correction, not over me—directly where my head had been. I stumbled, blinked, and nearly lost my balance. I reached down for the secret pouch I had been given by Azrael. I missed it at first attempt—the damn thing was invisible, after all. The demon spun, poison flinging from its claws. Or maybe it was my own blood.

It swiped again, seemingly faster than before. I ducked as the claws whizzed over me, then pulled back as they came back from the other direction. My own movements were supernaturally fast. They had to be. At the least, I was getting used to the demon's speed.

That was, until the other hand seemingly came out of nowhere, and raked through my neck and shoulder and sent me spinning to the ground, crying out louder than I wanted to admit. But damn, those claws hurt.

The demon obviously saw an opportunity and hurled himself at me recklessly. What it didn't see was that my left hand had found the hidden pouch and withdrawn a long, black sword. The Devil Killer. Or, in this case, the demon killer.

Or so I hoped.

I just brought the obsidian blade up as the demon descended down. I was surprised at how easily the sword slid into its chest, with seemingly no resistance at all. And I was most certainly surprised to discover that, in a puff of black, swirling smoke, the demon disappeared altogether. Hell, the sole indication that a demon had been here was the unholy mess of the place, and the burning wounds covering my body. The breakfast nook was demolished beyond recognition. A gaping hole was in the wall where the sliding glass door had been.

I dashed to Allison's side. She was out cold, the wound from her head still bleeding. I was momentarily distracted by all her blood. But I powered through, took her up in my arms, and over to the massive U-shaped couch. I hoped like hell she was okay, but the screeching coming from the foyer had my attention.

I set off down the hallway.

J.R. RAIN

20.

The foyer was mayhem.

The devil dog might have thought better about bursting into Kingsley's home, as the wolf and his monsters were holding their own. Indeed, the half-dozen Lichtenstein monsters veritably swarmed over it. The hellhound, easily as big as a rhino, was missing a partial head. Indeed, the left head had been cleaved in half, but you would never know it. Despite missing half its jaw and one of its burning eyes, it still snapped furiously. I watched it grab hold of Kingsley's gardener, a huge creation in his own right, and toss him head over ass across the foyer and into a table that had once sported a

Ming Dynasty vase that had long since been smashed to smithereens.

My son was nowhere to be found.

I was just about to shout his name when something flashed outside. Something massive and burning, and bringing down a flaming sword hard into what I could only assume was another demon. My son had left Kingsley and the monsters with the devil dog to fight the attacking demons. Alone.

I dashed through the melee, dodging the bodies of two Lichtenstein monsters who had been torn from limb to limb. As I ran, I watched Kingsley leap forward and engage one of the massive heads. A deep gash had opened along his left side. Blood poured free, as did hanging chunks of meat. Three mute Lichtenstein monsters, along with Franklin, hurled themselves at the other dog heads, and as I ran, I saw an opportunity.

I hopped over a dismembered arm and dove toward the devil dog's widespread front paws. I rolled to my back and, sliding in a pool of blood, and drove the Devil Killer deep into the creature's chest. Black blood poured down on me and, as each of the creature's three heads screeched loud enough to wake the dead—which they just might have done—it disappeared in a puff of oily smoke.

The three Lichtenstein monsters tumbled down, their quarry having disappeared, and the sudden silence in the foyer was immediately filled by the racket outside. I dashed through the damaged wall...

And into hell.

***

The Fire Warrior—my son—who stood nearly fifteen feet tall, had been single-handedly holding off the demons. By my count, there were eight in total, although I was also highly aware the bastards could pop in and out of existence, too. How many there truly were, I didn't know.

And where the devil was, I didn't know that, either.

Nor did I care. Not right now.

My son, after all, had been taking the brunt of the attack. I watched even now as another demon dive-bombed at him, wings stretched wide, claws extended. I screamed his name, but my son was already moving, jumping and flipping, slashing with his fiery sword, a blow that sent the demon spinning away into the dark of night.

More demons came, and my son fended them off, a true expert in the sword, unlike me, who had just learned the basics. Then again, I had learned the hell out of the basics, too.

I also noted that Anthony's second swipe, an expert arching slash that should have cleaved the next attacking demon diagonally in half, only sent it tumbling over Kingsley's once-perfectly manicured lawn, tearing deep furrows in it as it went. My son could only *fend* the demons off. He could not *kill* them. Just like Kingsley and his monsters—they could only fight the devil dog, not kill it.

No, that was my job. My *new* job.

Samantha Moon, Demon Killer.

As I ran toward my son, and as he fended off another demon that had managed to rake its claws along the side of his head, an attack that clearly wounded my son, I summoned the single flame.

But this time, I didn't see Talos in it—or where I might next jump. No, this time, I saw within it a pair of beautiful black wings.

***

"They are my gift to you," said Azrael, when the Archangel Michael had disappeared. I was sad to see him go. "Then again, they sort of come with the territory."

"As Death's Shadow?"

"Yes."

"Like the sword and secret pouch," I said.

"Indeed."

"Are mine glowing too?" I asked, pulling open my collar and trying to get a look behind me. I could see nothing. No, wait, there was something... a curved line just under my shoulder blade, but that was all I could see. But there it was. For the first time in my life, I was tatted up. I wasn't sure how I felt about that.

"By necessity, yours will appear as tattoos."

"I can see that. But they are, in fact, wings?"

"Wings in waiting, yes. Wings that need only to be summoned."

"After I disrobe?"

"Not quite, Sam. These are angel wings."

"So, I will be part angel, after all!"

"If it helps you, yes. As angel wings, they will not be part of your physical body."

"You lost me."

"Observe," he said, and he turned his back to me. As he did so, his glowing neon tattoo in the shape of a magnificent pair of wings, caught fire. Or so I thought. What it did was flare brightly and erupt into a beautiful set of golden wings. He flapped them lightly, lifting off the ground a foot or two. "Look again,

Sam."

I did, and saw what he meant. The joints of the wings were not attached to his skin, or what passed as his skin. The wings sort of hovered just above his skin. A part of him, yes, but separate too. I saw the genius of it immediately.

"Means I don't have to disrobe every time, doesn't it?"

"Indeed. The wings will hover over skin or clothing."

I nodded, relieved. I didn't want to battle demons and devils with my goods hanging out. The mental image of it nearly made me chuckle. That was, until I focused on the part of battling demons and devils.

He settled back to the floor and his wings once again folded in on themselves in a manner that suggested I'd long since gone nutso. "Now, let's see yours, Sam."

"What do I say?"

"You don't say anything. Imagine them there behind you. See them in your mind."

I imagined a pair of wings rising up behind me as beautiful as Azrael's, except mine were black and kind of bad-ass. But I felt nothing. I imagined harder. I imagined the shit out of those wings... but still, nothing.

"Don't hurt yourself, Sam. The wings are there, waiting."

I tried to really picture them in my mind. I saw myself flapping around in them, like a giant vampire tooth fairy. Nada. And while Azrael waited patiently, I realized he didn't know how to help me. Not really. The beautiful Angel of Death had been flying, perhaps, for all eternity. Sprouting wings came second nature to him. I wondered if he'd ever had a girlfriend. Or had made love.

Focus, Sam.

I considered what to do, growing more frustrated, until I realized growing frustrated didn't help. I calmed my mind, took a few steadying breaths, and the image of a flame came to mind. Not the actual flame that I summoned, but the idea of it. Could it work? I didn't know. Worth a shot.

And so, with the archangel gazing serenely upon me, I summoned the single flame, and within the flame, I saw a pair of beautiful black raven wings. I saw them flapping. And as they flapped, I felt myself rush toward them, and them to me. I gasped and stumbled.

Behind me rose a shadow. No, two shadows. Two massive and beautiful shadows.

"Very good, Sam. Now, shall we fly?"

***

The wings unfurled instantly, catching the wind like sails.

The feeling of their sudden appearance was unlike anything I'd experienced before. Although brand new, they felt like old friends. In fact, I would learn during my flight training with Azrael that the wings were an extension of my own soul. Even wilder, I would learn—and experience—the wings responding instant-aneously to my thoughts. I was truly one with them.

Perhaps most reassuring of all was that I wasn't running out here bare-breasted.

Thank God for that.

Now, to either side of me stretched uncommonly long, infinitely black wings, a fusion of physical and spiritual. Wings that were in this world, but not of this world. And if there were feathers, I couldn't see them. Truth was, I wasn't one hundred percent sure how I felt about sprouting feathers.

As I ran, I felt the wings catch the air, and divert it down. The force was undeniable and soon my running legs were only lightly touching Kingsley's crushed-shell driveway. And then only my toes were tapping—and then I was airborne...

And then, I was stumbling again, scraping a knee, momentarily dragging both my feet. I nearly did a barrel roll but somehow kept it together. My wings instinctively tucked in as I tumbled. Thank God for that. I would hate to damage them already.

I rolled up to my feet and was running again, but this time, I gave the wings a mighty flap, and now, I really was airborne. A foot off the ground, another foot. And I was flying.

Really flying.

***

"Good, Sam. Good. Bank left. Now right. Very good."

I did as he was told, still reeling from the rapturous, glorious, heady high of actually flying. Yes, I had flown with Talos often. But those had been his wings, his body. Although the sensation had been mind-blowing in its own right, it did not compare to flying in this body. This human/vampire/angel hybrid of a body. Me, Samantha Moon. Me, mother of two. Me, a private eye in Orange County. Me, a daughter and sister and friend and coffee addict. Me, flying. Here, in this hallway between worlds.

The Archangel Azrael watched me from below, calling out his commands.

"Now stop."

"I don't know how to stop."

"Stop flapping your wings."

"I don't know how to stop flapping my wings."

Indeed, I felt a bit like an out-of-control skier on the kiddie slope for the first time. Except this kiddie slope was many dozens of feet off the ground, and I was going far too fast.

"Stop, Sam."

"I don't know how—"

I veered off a pillar and spun out of control, slamming into the floor, tumbling and skidding. As I picked myself up, a glorious, massive, white silhouette appeared above me, smiling down.

"That is one way to stop. Are you okay?"

"I've been better." I stood, noting my wings were unscathed, despite my inglorious landing. I tasted blood in my mouth, although the wound was already healing.

When my head had cleared, I tried again, this time flying slower and more cautiously. Later, with more practice, I was able to stop. Not in midair. Not even Talos could stop in midair. But I could stop flapping, and glide, and learn to alight on my feet smoothly. Which I did, over and over.

Azrael also taught me how to run and fly, like an airplane on a runway. He also taught me how to leap up and gain altitude from a standing position. I had done my best to be a good student. Whether or not I lived through the night remained to be seen...

***

Trial by fire, I thought, as I gained altitude.

After all, this was my first flight in the real world—and it just so happened to be in the middle of a showdown with the devil and his spawn.

I counted eight of them, each as big as the next, and each sporting burning eyes and their own set of black wings. Had Kingsley had any neighbors, I suspect the police would have been called out long ago. I also suspected there might have been a heart attack or two in the neighborhood. As it was, Kingsley was a mile away from his neighbors' prying eyes.

From up here, I could see the deep grooves in his manicured lawn, the destruction of trees and hedges, and a demon shape burning in his backyard. How long my son could hold off the bastards, I didn't know, but there he was, slashing at yet another and another, sending each tumbling through the air. One landed on Kingsley's golf cart, obliterating it. Another crashed in the driveway fountain, shattering it.

Now, my son seemed to see me, and his

sword paused momentarily, and as it did, a demon raked across his face. My son roared and shook his head. He was wounded, that much was clear. But with all the fire, it was hard to tell. Another demon dashed toward him, its black claws extended. Aimed at my son's exposed back.

I knew this wasn't my son's back. It was the Fire Warrior's back, the warrior he became. But should the warrior perish, I knew my own son would be trapped in whatever world he temporarily found himself in.

Which, of course, wasn't going to happen.

I wasn't sure just how fast these wings could take me, but I was about to find out. In a blink, I found myself flying faster than I had ever before, so fast that I was completely out of control. And still, I flapped harder, holding the sword in my right hand. I felt like a jousting knight, except my opponent was a demon flashing toward my son, claws outstretched, ready to kill or maim, and I couldn't have either.

Not ever.

***

"I think you are ready, Sam."
"To fight the devil and his legion of

demons?"

"You are stronger than you think, and the angels will be watching over you."

"Helping me?"

"When possible. We cannot intervene directly."

"If you can't intervene between the devil and mankind, when can you intervene?"

"I'm sorry. This is not our fight. But we will be there, helping in subtle ways."

"I guess I'll just have to take what I can get."

"Yes. Now, you should go."

"Because we are done here?" I asked.

Azrael kept his gaze on me, his beautiful unwavering gaze, and said, "No, Sam. Because the devil is coming."

***

The demon and I converged.

Lucky for me, the demon had been intent on his target—my son. Unlucky for the demon, my sword was true. As it prepared to deliver a blow, the black emptiness of its chest was exposed, and I drove the sword deep within it. I caught a brief glimpse of its fiery eyes flaring, then extinguishing before it disappeared in a cloud of smoke. I smashed into the grass so hard that I was sure I had been broken a bone or two. Or three.

When I was done skidding on my face, I rose up on my knees, spitting sod and grit and blood. A quick check confirmed that my collarbone might be broken, but already, it was healing.

I stood on shaking legs, my wings providing me balance. My son had turned and moved toward me. In fact, he was reaching out a hand toward me. Thank God he could still see. But I was reluctant to grab his oversized hand, mostly because it was burning continuously. Hell, I could feel the heat. How the grass around his feet didn't catch fire, I didn't entirely know. No one knew. It was a mystery in and of itself. Kingsley had tried to explain it away that my son existed within a sort of gravitational field, a sort of bubble. If that was true, then how could I feel the heat of him now? And where was the damn bubble? His striking sword sure as hell sent the demons tumbling.

Anyway... a moot point.

My son watched me—and, for all I knew, stared at me. He was seeing my wings for the first time and I sensed his wonder. Something flashed above us, and he spun faster than something that big and burning had any right to spin. His sword came around in a great, sweeping, blazing arc, and the attacking demon was driven straight into the ground—and very close to me.

With a yell that would do the Amazons of Themyscira proud, I leaped high and plunged my sword with hands down into its demon's black, swirling chest. It screeched, contorted, and disappeared.

Another appeared behind me—either materializing out of thin air or swooping down without detection. Luckily, my own inner alarm blared so loud that I automatically ducked without knowing what was happening. A rush of wind passed over me. In fact, I think it passed *through* my wings themselves. Luckily, my wings were there but not there.

I spun, swinging my sword blindly, and clashed loudly with spiked claws. Unfortunately, my sword didn't do any damage to the claws. In fact, it only seemed to anger the demon, who literally grew in size before me.

I endured a hellish barrage from its hacking, swiping, cutting, slicing claws, some of which landed home, sending me spinning and tumbling and crying out. The demon claws burned worse than silver. Hell, maybe they were made partially with silver.

Another swipe, and I felt a chunk of flesh hacked off my chin. Another swipe and I watched some of my dark hair flutter to the grass. Another swipe, and this time, I parried nicely. The second set of claws came and I ducked, and spun on a knee, saw my opening, and drove my sword up into its chest, and watched with satisfaction as its furnace-like eyes died out.

Nearby, my son backhanded another demon so hard that he sent it through a fence. Soon, my son and I were working in tandem, him using his brute strength and unparalleled skill to send the demons if not quite back to hell, definitely down into Kingsley's much-maligned and once-beautiful front yard landscaping.

And that's where I waited, plunging with glee, not feeling bad at all that most of the demons were dazed and a little confused. *They attack my son, Fire Warrior or not, and they are going to die.* It was the simplest pop math quiz ever. Attacking my son equaled death.

We did this, over and over, until there were none.

Both my son and I scanned the heavens, the shadows, anywhere and everywhere, but nothing materialized. Near the house, I watched some of the Lichtenstein monsters approach; the wolf, too. Kingsley had been damaged. Or, rather, his inner wolf counterpart had. I could see the bloody gashes from here. It was a wonder that the wolf was alive. The thought of losing Kingsley was terrible to comprehend. I knew that Kingsley and the wolf were truly one. There really was an inner wolf within him. He didn't summon it from another world. If the wolf was hurt, he was hurt. Perhaps even too hurt to transform. I knew the feeling; my own wounds were reluctant to heal.

The wolf made an effort to come to us, but Franklin put a hand on it, keeping it at bay. Not a bad idea. Kingsley was too hurt to do much. Besides, the demons appeared to be gone. For now.

My son stepped over to me, and lowered his sword. His burning skin crackled and spat. I could have been next to the world's biggest bonfire. A true Burning Man. We continued scanning the surroundings. Both of us, I suspected, knew that all was too calm. Too quiet.

Also, my inner alarm hadn't stopped buzzing. In fact, it had even begun to pick up in intensity.

Footsteps. Near the front gate. Both my son and I snapped our heads around. Now, the sound of hands clapping. Kingsley's front gate, amazingly, was still closed. Then again, when demons could materialize in the sky overhead, a front gate became a moot point.

A middle-aged man in a black suit stepped out of the shadows, still clapping and maybe even laughing. Hard to tell from where we were. He clapped all the way to the front gate. Without missing a beat, he did something with his hands, and the wrought-iron fence exploded inward, wrenching free from its hinges and landing in a pile of twisted metal and dust, literally shaking the earth beneath my feet.

The devil was here.

21.

The man kicked aside the gate, and it went skittering over the gravel as surely as if he'd kicked a tin can.

To my utter surprise, three Lichtenstein monsters charged past us. Like the demons, they protected their master. As they dashed forward, one loping and another flat-out limping, I saw the well-dressed man grin. I also saw him reach inside his jacket and remove something that gleamed dully. Two daggers. Silver daggers.

The first Lichtenstein monster was upon

him. I knew him well. His name was Gerald and he was, perhaps, the politest of all the monsters, and spoke with a crisp English accent. Now, he roared and hurled himself through the air, leaping easily twenty feet or more. Not to my surprise, the man in black dashed forward, too, leaping as well. The two met in mid-air, and the roar I had heard quickly turned to a strangled cry. When the two landed, only one did so smoothly on his feet; the other thudded on his back, unmoving, a dagger protruding from his chest.

The man in black smiled and adjusted his sleeves, rolled his neck a little. I could hear it crack from here.

The next two Lichtenstein monsters leaped —both gardeners here at the estate, and both with whom I'd had little contact. Both were obviously devoted to Kingsley to the end. And their end came quickly. With a flurry of feet and hands, a cacophony of grunts and strangled cries, two heads fell free. Both bounced, rolled, and came to a stop, as their massive, headless bodies finally toppled next to them. The devil had barely broken stride.

He continued down the driveway, whistling. Another Lichtenstein monster appeared. And another. Both monsters were quickly dispatched. Both had been kind to me. Both had been family, in their own way—especially to Kingsley this past year. Both had died trying to protect him. Enough of this. Enough.

Kingsley the wolf would be no match for what I saw coming at us, especially in his condition. Neither would Franklin, nor the remaining two Lichtenstein monsters—all of whom would be summarily dispatched.

"Your son is impressive, Samantha Moon," said the man, raising his voice as he approached. "You should be proud. Then again, you turned him, didn't you? Your selfish act made him the monster he is today. The freak he will be for all eternity." The devil bowed. "I commend you, Sam. In all the history of the world, rarely have I seen a worse mother. In fact, you might hold the crown."

Don't let him get to you, Sam, came Allison's thoughts into my head.

I turned and saw her next to Kingsley, holding her head. Blood ran between her fingers.

Are you okay?

Don't worry about me. I've got your back.

"And don't even get me started on your daughter, Samantha," said the devil, walking toward me. The possessed man's tie whipped crazily in the wind. I noted the fresh blood on his shirt. "Now, had you done your job—a job any mother would have done, mind you—you would have spared your family. You would have fled for the hills, or to the graveyards, or wherever your filthy kind congregate. You would have faked your death, or, even better, plunged a silver dagger into your own chest and rid the world of the problem—the very real problem—you have become."

Sam, look, came Allison's voice in my head.

I turned and saw where she was pointing into the sky. I saw a flash appear and disappear. Many flashes. They were angels, and one of them, I was certain, had been Ishmael. They were nearby. How they were helping, I didn't know. But I found their presence comforting.

"Oh, you see them, too. Whew, I thought I was going a little crazy. I thought maybe this new body—and mind—was a dud. Your angels can only do so much, Samantha Moon. They know, and I know, that we are bound in this moment. This is not their fight. This is our fight."

More flashing from high above, but that's where the flashing stayed—high above.

"So much centers around you. You are, in fact, the key that could unlock untold destruction into this world. Through you, the dark masters can rise again. And yet, here you stand, with your new wings and your new sword, a brave little girl with her monstrous son nearby, and her freak of a daughter not too far away at all. Yes, I can hear her, Sam. And I can hear her listening in on your thoughts, too. By proxy, I can follow your own train of thoughts, Sam. Oh, you didn't know that? Why else would I need your daughter, Sam Moon? Oh, I see that my words are getting to you. Good. They should. They would get to anyone with a conscience. Do yourself a favor and put down the sword. Better yet, give it to me. I'm really, really not sure what I was thinking by conceding to its creation. A rare lapse in judgment."

I wasn't sure what to say, or how to respond. Were his words getting to me? I tried to think they weren't, but I knew there was truth to them.

He stepped closer, moving slowly, and I could see now the evil grin plastered on his face, wide as ever. The man, whoever he was, had been thoroughly and completely possessed. Even worse, he'd invited the devil in.

"Yes," came the devil's words, following my train of thought via my daughter. "He worshiped me for only a few months. Sadly, he thought it was all a joke. I rarely joke, Sam."

I gripped the sword more tightly in my hand. Next to me, my giant of a son shifted on his own feet.

"Lay down the weapon, Sam, and let me rid the world of the scourge that is you. Consider it a favor. I'll do what you didn't have the guts to do, and the dark masters will have to wait for their next chosen one."

The devil stepped closer, and now, I could see the fire in his pupils, even from here.

"Yes, Sam. Our paths have crossed. Of course, I had known this day was coming. I just hadn't known with whom. Oh, how I was disappointed to discover it would be with a bored, confused, suburban housewife. A private eye, no less. And a vampire, of all things. Then again, I should have known it would be a filthy bloodsucker. Few could have found the sword. And, yes, there it is. And there are your wings. I suppose crossing paths with a vampire makes some sense. A shame I will have to kill you in front of your son, and with your daughter listening in, as well. Surely, they will be scarred for life."

My son stepped forward. He'd apparently had enough. He raised his burning sword, which crackled and spit fire and looked for all the world like something straight out of a *Mummy* movie.

The devil paused, grinned even wider— while at the same time, I saw a brief flash of fear cross the man's eyes. Now the man raised his silver dagger—and slashed it across his own throat. He dropped, choking and gagging and spitting up blood. Now kicking and flopping. The slash had been too deep to help the man, even if I had been inclined to do so. I hadn't. And, as he flopped, a swirling, black, inky shadow rose up, a shadow that somehow also gleamed wetly. It spun and twisted and took shape.

The shadow continued to grow and morph. It turned and undulated in the air, taking on more depth and detail, and for the span of time it took for the flopping man to finally die, there stood before us the devil.

The real devil. As he appeared when not possessing mankind.

Azrael had prepared me for what to expect, but nothing—nothing—could prepare me for this. Nothing. Not ever.

***

The devil stood twenty feet or more, clearly taller than my son, himself a giant. Definitely taller than the demons he had created.

I briefly considered summoning Talos, just so that I could match the devil's size, but I knew that even Talos did not possess the weaponry—or fortitude—to overcome or withstand what I was seeing before me.

The devil, I knew, had never been truly tested, until now.

Lucky me.

Except what I saw before me—a hulking, grotesque, burning nightmare—was enough to make me run for the nearby hills and never look back. The burning eyes, now as big as bonfires, could have been doorways into hell itself. The massive, twisted horns belonged on something prehistoric and terrible. Its many claws looked like real scythes, only bigger, and each was as black as night. Unlike his demons, the devil sported veins of glowing fire that crackled upon his black skin. Real skin, too, unlike his demons who had seemed more shadow than substance. More than anything, the thing before me seemed unstoppable. More so than the giant worm I had encountered. Or even the dragon from earlier in the week. The demons, although fierce and filled with hate, had appeared waif-like. The devil dog had been terrible to behold, but it had been a good deal smaller than this thing. Indeed, what I saw before me could destroy whole cities, whole nations, and never stop destroying until the Earth had been laid to waste.

I stood there, unable to move, barely able to

think.

That is, until my son stepped between myself and the devil, and raised his sword.

***

The blur of the attack was mind-boggling. The devil came at my son with claws slashing, and my son met each claw with his flashing sword, a sword that moved in blurred arcs, as fast as a spinning top.

At one point, my son stepped back, raised his free hand, and summoned another flaming sword. The battle resumed anew, and the two entities fought in a seemingly choreographed ballet of death. Each swipe, each thrust, each slash were all blocked by both fighters, all done with a speedy damage that I could barely follow. For each move, there was a counter-move, for each step backward, there was a step forward. For each attack, there was a perfectly timed counterattack.

If my son was wearing out, I couldn't tell. If he was slowing down, I didn't see it. All done at such a high level of skill and precision and, oddly, in unison, that I was left immobile, speechless, and filled with untold fear. This was my son, after all, fighting the devil in his rawest, most hideous form. A devil unleashed.

There was a pause in action—and I immediately saw why. One of the devil's long, curved, claws had found an opening. And that opening was through my son's shoulder. Indeed, the curved devil tusk had punched through the fire, and out the other side.

My son drove his fist—and the pommel of his burning sword—into the devil's hideous face, slid off the black claw and stumbled backward. Molten lava poured from the wound in his shoulder. The devil's own blazing eyes widened with what could only be pleasure, and as he raised his clawed hand for what would surely be the end of my son, I dashed forward, spread my wings, and took flight.

***

A fireball appeared over my shoulder, and slammed into the devil, who staggered backward.

I turned back and saw Allison running from the house, arms raised. More fire erupted in her hands and she hurled it forward. The fireballs sailed past me in a blink and exploded in the devil's face. The massive, hoofed creature staggered back and clawed at his burning face.

As another fireball just missed my outstretched wing and slammed into the devil's shoulder, sending him spinning, I made a mental note to compliment Allison on her aim. That was, if I survived the night. I also briefly wondered if the surrounding angels had anything to do with Allison's aim.

Those thoughts were fleeting and instant. For now, I raised my sword and flew as fast as I could, praying like hell that one of Allison's projectiles didn't hit me in the ass.

Suddenly, another demon appeared before me. It raked me across the face, and sent me tumbling to the grass below.

From the ground, I looked up—and watched as demon after demon popped into existence. Dozens of them. Hundreds, in fact.

The devil threw back his monstrous head and laughed.

***

Many of them formed a barrier around the devil, a black shield of claws and burning, red eyes.

Across the yard, Kingsley had Allison, looking like a girl with her giant dog. Nearby, my son struggled to stand, and I suspected the poison from the devil's claws was working its way through him. Above, demons gathered in a swirling swarm. They weren't about to let their devil—their master—die without a fight.

"Block your thoughts, baby," I whispered to my daughter, praying like hell she was still safe in the cell, and still listening to me. "Don't let the devil know what Mommy is about to do next."

It was time to end this. I gathered my strength and launched straight up into the night air, even as the demons oriented on me, flashing forward, claws raised. Through it all, a plan began to form in my mind.

A terrible plan, granted. But a plan, nonetheless.

***

A demon appeared before me and swiped with its claws. I parried, lost my balance, nearly plummeted, and righted myself.

Another demon, another clash. Its claw found my throat, and I felt the skin open up and blood pump out. Had I needed to breathe, I would have been dead.

The devil watched all of this from behind his swarm of red-eyed creations. His expression was unfathomable, but I sensed his unease. He should feel uneasy. After all, as the next demon swooped down, claws ready to strike, I summoned the single flame—and saw within it the only place on this Earth that could end this madness.

***

Within the flame, I felt myself rushing to this place, and just as something swiped where my head had been, I found myself in another location altogether.

A space just in front of the devil's massive, heaving, black, molten chest. A space just inside his ring of protective demons.

The devil reared back at my sudden appearance—evidence that my daughter had kept the bastard in the dark. He roared and reached up as if to swat a mosquito away. Except this mosquito was armed to the teeth.

With all my might, I plunged the Devil Killer deep into its swirling black and fiery chest. All the way to the hilt.

His swatting, clawed hand paused in mid-swat, and he looked down with burning eyes at the sword handle protruding from his chest. He looked back at me, and almost appeared to smile, but what I did know? As the devil began to drop, he also began fading away. Except this time, no inky, oily black smoke rose up from him. Nothing rose up at all. The devil disappeared completely.

One by one, the demons, who looked on, winked out of existence. They were not dead, I knew. Their connection to their master was gone. Unbound, they, too, disappeared. I suspected I would meet them again someday. Each and every one of them.

I alighted on the grass, where I found the Devil Killer protruding like an arrow in a bullseye. I took it up, and re-sheathed it in my secret pouch. I summoned the single flame again, and within it, I watched my wings fold in on themselves. In the real world, they did exactly that, too. Somewhere on my back was the mother of all tramp stamps. Two of them.

There were dead Lichtenstein monsters everywhere, and before me, the Fire Warrior had taken a knee, holding his shoulder. A short while later, my son was in his place, kneeling similarly. He stood, momentarily confused, and touched where the wound had been, but it was gone, of course. Indeed, it was the Fire Warrior who had been gravely wounded.

My son spotted me and rushed over and threw his arms around me, weeping harder than I'd ever seen him weep. And soon, my own tears were flowing. Now here was Allison, wrapping her arms around both of us. I called out to Tammy, and soon heard her running across the gravel, accompanied by the Lichtenstein monster who had been guarding her. A still-injured Kingsley swooped her up in his massive arms and joined us.

All around us, beautiful angels dropped from the sky. They landed on bent knees, wings outstretched. Closest to me was Ishmael, who rose to his full height, nearly as tall as Azrael, but not quite. He caught my eye and nodded.

Somewhere, nearby, sirens blared.

The End

About the Author:

J.R. Rain is an ex-private investigator who now writes full-time. He lives in a small house on a small island with his small dog, Sadie. Please visit him at www.jrrain.com.

CPSIA information can be obtained
at www.ICGtesting.com
Printed in the USA
LVHW081749101218
599924LV00020B/1453/P

9 781548 255190